by FIELDING DAWSON

Criticism

An Essay on New American Fiction
The Man in the Dark Blue Suit
Entelechy One

Stories & Dreams

Krazy Kat/The Unveiling
The Dream/Thunder Road
The Sun Rises Into The Sky

Memoirs

An Emotional Memoir of Franz Kline
The Black Mountain Book (A Memoir of the College)

Novels

Open Road
The Mandalay Dream
A *Great* Day for a Ballgame

Novellas

Elizabeth Constantine
Thread
The Greatest Story Ever Told/A Transformation

THE SUN
RISES
INTO
THE SKY

And Other Stories
1952-1966

FIELDING
DAWSON

1974
BLACK SPARROW PRESS
Los Angeles

Some of these stories have appeared in the following magazines: *Center, Fervent Valley, For Now, Lines, Move, Shortstop, Wild Dog*. The story "There Is a Man 1 Know" was later re-written, and appears as the opening section of a novel, *The Mandalay Dream*, under the title "Entelechy One" (Bobbs-Merrill, 1972).

The cover collage is by the author.

LIBRARY OF CONGRESS CATALOGING IN PUBLICATION DATA

Dawson, Fielding, 1930-
    The sun rises into the sky.

    I. Title.
PZ4.D27235Su [PS3554.A948]   813'.5'4   73-15891
ISBN 0-87685-115-4
ISBN 0-87685-114-6 (pbk.)

This Book is for the Poets

"Where there is no love, there is no art."
—Paracelsus

AUTHOR'S INTRODUCTION

THIS BOOK, which I was temped to call a novel, completed a circle which began with the writing of the story "Krazy Kat" at Black Mountain, and ended with the title story here; I had developed a prototype.

But the work I had ahead of me, the change I was unwittingly—and unwillingly—approaching, hit and stayed with me regardless of how I felt or regarded my own writing, and it was my memoir of my relationship with the artist Franz Kline, followed by *The Black Mountain Book*, that was the evidence that I had changed from a third person metaphor to the first person-actual prose; proof being that the Kline Memoir germinated within the last few sections—the naked ones—in this book, and that means that this book, while fulfilling a whole phase or circle in my life, yet paved the way to a new prose, and a fresh attitude.

Facts can make you weary—but, anyway, in the mid 1960s, I was in a despair where the only way out was through the bottom, which was where I went, so it must be a fact of sorts—a creative fact—that because of the intensity of the battle of my selves—light and dark—some of the best (dark), and worst (light), prose I've ever written, was done then, as I believe this book, along with its companions, *Krazy Kat/The Unveiling* and *The Dream/Thunder Road*, shows.

In the future you might miss—and fear I'll have lost—that lyrical and often strange dark spirit found in my past prose surface. But neither the surface nor even the story—the all—of "Red Impact," or "Hey There! All you People," can be repeated. It happened that way. I was there. I saw it, reached for it, and got it—got *two*.

There was a way I was in a bar with a glass of beer in front of me in those days and nights that held civilization in suspense; *every motion was conscious and vital*. All the effects crystallized, as in a dream, and it was very much a dream, and when I saw the city out the door and a woman played the juke-box and the music came on, I was involved with the essence of all things. The writer must know the rhythm of the mundane as the origin of suspense.

So, somewhere along in the future, if you miss that certain something in my prose, think of me, because I will too. But, life being what it is, what was was, in the natural elements of change, and for me it is the loss of Hell—*that* Hell I mean, the one that was, where I knew the rules I could (and did) break. Not the one coming up, where if there are any rules, I don't know them, and they wouldn't help me if I did, which no doubt, I shall reflect on years hence, as I do here. But! there is one rule—conscious, with a hard core, that will help: don't hurt with vision. Don't use perception vicariously as a whip. So then, I intend to hurt no one, here; the full circle that this book embodies seems but merely in its appointed place, continually responding, and that being the situation, see how frightening change really is, why the sad trembling mob crouches at the bottom of the wall hoping it all blows over like it used to in the crib. Change is pain and synonym for Hell, and nobody wants it, but everybody wants what comes afterwards. I feel a kind of low laugh—they think it's bliss, lots of money, color TV and the rest of that associational toyland junk that pollutes our savage unconscious, and what they miss is the clear, clean-air magic that follows change, in life and art, that's found in the scent of a discovery of a higher suspense. The suspense involved in a more expanding change. The true light comes up through the darkness. I'm a cadmium yellow chameleon. And, a writer who is emotionally honestly in terror of the changes he or she must and will make, but who yet *loves* suspense, ought to be able, it seems to me, to write a pretty good story.

Fielding Dawson
July 1973
New York

TABLE OF CONTENTS

FOUR EARLY STORIES

A NOTE ON *FOUR EARLY STORIES*

I LIKE these stories very much.

"High and High Spade" was written in the spring of 1953, at Black Mountain College. "Salad" was written in the spring of '52 at school, and when I gave a reading of my new work there, around May of '52, I read it along with some other things, including a wild little story which I in no way understood, but which I thought strange, stimulating, desperate, original, and really wonderful. But maybe I was desperate—anyway, the story was called "Krazy Kat," and I loved it, yet I thought "Salad" was better, so when I read, I saved it for last, and as I was reading "Krazy Kat" out loud, or, just as I read the next to last sentence, which is a question, *What did you make,* Charley Olson jumped forward in his chair, he was sitting right in front of me, and before I could read the last sentence, he cried out, *A Tiger!* and, so, well my favorite story "Salad" seemed like a salad indeed, straight cabbage; after that Tiger.

I thought I'd lost these stories in a fire in New York in the winter of 1959-60, but last summer in Colorado, my sister gave them to me. I re-read them, and found myself *really* liking "Salad"! Well! There it was again! These old leaves refuse to die! I was pleased, and very deeply, to see the original places and feel the tone of my first novel *Open Road,* to be reading dialogue by a girl I later named Daisy Woolworth, and who then, at Black Mountain, when I was twenty-one, was myself as she (I) was and would also be later on in writing that novel.

"The Tin Angel" (à la "Krazy Kat," but which ends in a bop joke and bop jokes fascinated me), was written in 1953, at school. The fellow named Peter Engelland is in truth a man named John Kaspar, who, being a disciple of Pound's, was involved in Frobenius in that stern and pedantic way Pound's disciples had, and I met Kaspar when he visited school. Kaspar became very famous, infamous in fact, in the late 1950s. Most black people around my age (42) will remember him, but if you're white, and ask, be careful.

"At the Farm" was written in October of '52, and was influenced by Faulkner and the patient repetitive Kalahari Bushmen prose which was brought into English (or into German and then English), by a missionary named W. H. I. Bleek, around 1890, that I went to The Library of Congress to copy, and did copy, some Bushmen Tales (see my story "Reflections of Steel"). I went to D. C. after the summer session of 1950, and stayed with Neil and Ken Noland while I copied the material. "At the Farm" has a smart-student quality of writing, but is important to me, because with "Salad," there was an effort toward a non-metaphorical prose, and in these four short stories a clear double prose direction is evident, and the strength of both directions was a lasting one, carrying clear up to the present, almost, on the one hand an internal quarrel (see the passage Dear Papa in *The Mandalay Dream*), voiced in a descriptive prose, and here, in "High and High Spade," and "The Tin Angel," in a stilted 19th Century prose, while the other two stories, far more relaxed, have a spatial and energetic even talking quality that beckons—twenty years later— more than ever. A perceptive prose with that monosyllabic directness in Dashiell Hammett. But Faulkner was a little in my ear then, and an influence.

Yet "Krazy Kat" seemed, in a puzzling way, to have both, or to try at both, or maybe it overwhelmed any direction, but no matter, because it influenced me, and as the student writing was intense and of high quality (we were writing of the experience of Black Mountain—and ourselves: pretty fierce), in some way I felt that "Krazy Kat," always to me a schoolroom

(14)

discussion of Blake's poem "The Tiger," yet held a quality of suspense in that *something was certain to follow*, and as intuitive as "Krazy Kat" was, I was intuitively aware that there was a prose that would follow it, and possibly the voices and the energy in the clear dialogic prose of "Salad" and "At the Farm" held the clue; *The Black Mountain Book*.

So, "Krazy Kat" was in a sense the key. I don't know how, but in the dialogue, and the sense that something must follow, I *in those days* let my own story influence me. How audacious could I get?

But—what the hell! I knew it was good, and if I could be influenced by my story, great! Because what that meant was I was responding to myself and my work, which made the foundation strong, and just before I was drafted, in August of '53, my future felt like a real place to be.

I'd like to dedicate these four stories to Jack Rice, who, at a party one night when we were really drunk—another of those grim deep purple parties we had at school—told me, in so few words, about myself. Jack had been at that reading, and had responded in a positive way that had shaken me, and at that party months after the reading, told me about my future with a warmth and power—in his voice, that I then determined to make my own.

September 26, 1972

AT THE FARM

THE SERIES WAS OVER. The Yankees beat the Dodgers. It began to rain and Barnes came across the field till he got to where I was standing. He said it's raining and I said, Yes, it's raining but I was thinking what Joe would say at supper. I was laughing to myself about Cleveland. I told Barnes the Yanks won and he said Oh really? and I said yes and he didn't care because I was thinking they won The Series: The Yanks Have Won The Series like in a story the name the title but like it was them winning The Series in headline I could smell that paper and Barnes said as he held out his hand with his palm up he said it's raining but doesn't it smell nice and I grinned and said Yes and then he asked me what we should be doing and I pointed at the rows of plowed up potatoes and said

We should be picking those up.

With what?

Our hands.

Where do they go?

In baskets.

Baskets? Where are they?

At the end of the field. I pointed. Over there. He got some. I saw Jines drive the tractor into the shed. I thought he looked like Floyd, a little, but different because Floyd looks more loose on the tractor and comfortable. Jines came walking out and went to bring the cows down to be milked.

Some of the potatoes are little, some are big, they grow in clumps and like Barnes said you can walk ten feet and not find a potato and then find a dozen. It was not Barnes who said that it was Gus. Barnes picked up a basket and so did I and we began at one end of the row and we picked up potatoes and put the full baskets up by the road so they could be picked up with the truck and then we began with new baskets on a new row and we got them filled too, and then Barnes asked me what to do next and I said,

Now we rake.

What is that?

At the end of the row there's a potato fork and you get that. There's one missing. I'll get another at the barn, Dole said there's one around somewhere. You rake at the side of the furrow, you just rake the loose dirt, break up the clumps and look for potatoes. It's not hard but it's something.

Okay.

I'll go and try and find the fork now. You go ahead. I'll get back soon.

He went to the end of the row to get the fork that was lying there and I went to the other end of the field to the barn awhile and couldn't find it so I went down the road and turned by the fence by the ditch and I looked under Dole's house and then, by the trees, I saw a long handle. It wasn't a fork it was a hoe and I thought that I would use that as well and I took that and cut across the field from the house to where Barnes was standing raking and he was doing it all wrong so I showed him how to do it and he said,

Oh yes, that's a good way, too.

It began to let up a little but then rained harder. Barnes said that it was raining harder than before and I said, Yes, it is. Dole came down the road in his Ford and turned into the yard in front of his house and he stopped. He got out and came to where we were working and asked me if I found the rake.

No, I said.

Barnes said it was raining.

It sure is, Dole said. He looked at me.

Ain't it. I said,

It sure is. Dole said,

How much you done?

About two and a half rows.

That's good. Tomorrow we'll bring in some tobacco.

Then he went across the field to the house and Barnes and I watched him. I said that it must be near six and Barnes said he didn't know and I said, Well, when we finish this row, we'll quit and Barnes didn't say anything. He began raking potatoes and I did too and a little while later we put the hoe and fork under the house and walked down to supper and Barnes asked if this kind of weather keeps up for long down here and I said it sure does. You get used to it. It stays like this and when it's different it's snow and gets colder and after that it gets windy and blows out doors and windows. After that it gets hot and then like this again. Barnes frowned and said Jesus. He was from Boston.

THE NEXT DAY

The next day it was raining again and Floyd jumped up on the tractor and yelled TOOT TOOT and the tractor began to move ahead. Dole and I stood on the waggon in back. It was loaded with tobacco. Dole and I laughed and so did Cleary's father and Gus. Barnes walked up ahead to pull the threaded tobacco stakes up to put on the waggon to take to the barn where we would hang them and wait until it stopped raining. When the tobacco was cut the stalks were pushed over the gav which is a metal tip on the end of a stake, and when there are five or seven or eight stalks, the stake is pulled up, loaded on

(19)

the waggon and taken to be hung in the barn to dry and later the shriveled leaves are taken off the stakes and graded. But the tobacco barn wasn't finished yet and Dole was hanging the stakes full of tobacco in the cow barn, the beef stall and in the barn where I saw Buck given an injection for his bad eye. Floyd held Buck's head and they tied a rope around his neck and brought it around a beam and held the end of the rope and Floyd said, Buck's a good bull.

The waggon jerked a little from side to side as it went through the mud. Up ahead Gus and Cleary's father had a stake ready for us when the waggon slid to a stop. Floyd and Gus shouted at the tractor because it was still skidding on even after Floyd stopped it. But finally it stopped and Gus and Cleary's father handed the stake up to us and Dole told Cleary's father to be careful and Cleary's father sort of smiled, we took the stake with all the tobacco leaves threaded on it and we laid it very carefully like a tablecloth over the other stakes of leaves and we did it very carefully, not to injure the leaves. Then Barnes gave us a stake and then Cleary's father and then Gus and then Barnes again and Floyd got off the tractor and helped and so on until the waggon was piled high and we went to the barn. We sat in the doorway of the barn and looked out at the rain and big dark clouds hanging over the mountains that surrounded the valley. Dole said that turkeys are crazy. They follow you around and get in your way because they walk around in the rain. I could see Floyd looking out from the doorway across fields and he said to Dole,

You got company, Dole.

A car came skittering up the road pretty fast and slid into the yard in front of the house. I wondered if Cleary was there, the man was knocking on the door and then he quit and got in his car and we watched him back out and turn and drive up to the barn and stop in front of us. He got out and came toward us and nobody said anything. Then he said he was looking for the man that ran the farm for the College and Dole said,

That's me.

Floyd said at the same time, pointing at Dole, He's right there. Dole and the man talked a little, after the man introduced himself, about some custom work that he had to have done would Dole send somebody down sometime soon. Dole said that he would and smiled at Gus. Gus here would be down Tuesday morning. Then they squatted down on their haunches in the doorway of the barn and one of the turkeys got up and walked around on the hood of that man's car and Dole went over and it flew off and we laughed and Dole said they were ignorant things they always got in your way. Dole and the man talked about plowing and how hard plowing had been a few months before because of the drought and I watched the man roll a cigarette. He had blonde hair and a white shirt. Floyd was inside the barn tapping his hand on one of the steel bars that separated the cow stalls. He was back in the corner and I wondered if Floyd knew the blonde man. Floyd was all loose, tapping his hand on the steel bar waiting for Dole to stop.

The sun came out and the chickens and turkeys and guineas and bantys were walking around and Floyd rattled a chain on the bar and Dole said that field out there had been hard when they had plowed it and he asked Gus if he wasn't right and Gus said yep that was right and after the man had gone and when the tobacco had been put in and we were finishing up cutting corn and the sun was shining bright and the shadows were long across the floor of the valley I asked Floyd if he knew that man and he said no that he didn't know him, I don't know many people around here, I come from California. I thought of that bent license plate on his old Dodge as I looked at him and Floyd said he sure thought that man talked a lot.

THE TIN ANGEL

HE WAS QUITE TALL and had a mischievous look in his eyes, and he wore a long tweed overcoat, and when he introduced himself to me he put out his hand, and asked:

Have you read *The Voice of Africa?*

I introduced myself,

Yes, parts.

And.

Fine, except in parts it's dull then.

Ah, that was the style then.

His name was Peter Engelland and two years later when he came back he apologized for not returning my manuscripts.

I'm sorry, he said, listen I was so completely busy. I didn't know this from that—seriously. I got involved with printing the new book, back letters, correspondence, you know, and I really didn't *have* a second of my own.

Some months later he came back. I was eating and I looked up and, behind me, standing behind me, a little, grinning, there he was, and he shook my hand.

I thought the section on culture was awfully fine.

"The culture circle signifies every area of uniform culture." Marvelous. As he stayed, he walked around, thinking, about the lecture, make it exact, what he would say perfection, later, at Kenneth's.

At Kenneth's, he sat on the floor, beside a floor lamp so that the light from the circular cone of the lamp shade shone a little into his eye.

As you know, he began, much has been said of parallels between contemporary abstraction and Oriental esthetic, but the point is this.

At that point there was a knock on the door.

In come in, called Kenneth.

It was a messenger boy.

I have a wire for Kenneth Potter.

Yes, said Kenneth, I am here, here, he said, getting off the floor, come in, close the door.

The messenger boy gave the telegram to Kenneth.

$1.50, sir.

Kenneth paid the boy and the boy left.

What does it say?

KEN: SAIL TOMORROW AT TEN, PANSIES PERFUME FOR YOU FROM VIENNA—TOOTS.

Who's Toots.

Toots Robinson. Don't you remember—

Why you mean—

Oh get out.

There are supreme stages of content.

Of what?

Content.

Content.

Yes, content.

Well, it starts out—I'm going to go right into it—right away—itself—

But that isn't the whole—

Yes yes I understand.

But when I think about—

Yes but you don't start at the other end!

Never! That would give it away!

If a man has a patriotic song and a reasonable quantity of

rhetoric, how will he talk?

Indeed, if there is another face by which he displaces his own, which is he to call his?

What is the difference between a magician and a line of chorus girls.

The next day we went to the farm for a picnic. Peter, Carolyn, Kenneth, Phillip, Ann and myself. Ann had an uncle who owned some land outstate, and we drove out for the weekend.

The house was rather shabby. It was very dirty and it was falling in. The caretaker quit, Ann said, because everything was wrecked, and he was through taking care of a wrecked farm. There were no animals and the barn was sagging to one side. The chicken coop was completely finished. The weeds and brush were overgrown, grown over the paths and most of the porch.

Peter brought along a few books and was reading to Carolyn inside the kitchen. Phillip and Kenneth and Ann and myself went for a tour of the farm.

It was really very funny.

This is the corn, Ann said, waving her hands.

These are the grapes.

This is the watermelon patch.

Oh look, here are some weeds.

My uncle, Ann said, bought this property when he was 22 and he said it was good land then and that it is good land now.

We went back for lunch.

Carolyn had cleaned up things a little and made some lunch, and as we came in she smiled to us and Peter smiled and said

What we still have to learn—

Shut *up* Peter, said Phillip.

The water we had with the sandwiches was a little dirty,

coming from the broken cistern.

Look down there, said Ann.

Kenneth peered down into the well.

It's not very full nor does it seem clean.

After lunch we sat on the front porch.

Let's go for a walk. Who wants to go for a walk.

I do, said Carolyn.

Watch out for the snakes.

Oh God. Are there snakes here?

Why you mean you—listen, this place is known—

Now really! I'm not going to go.

No—go on. But just keep out of the tall grass.

What do you mean, why that's all this wretched place is!

I'll go by myself then.

He loves me he

What are you doing?

Loves me not he

I don't understand one part. What did he mean when he said the telegram.

He means that one he got last night—he told me about it then. It seems that it was a gind of cheap thing to do, yellow, and he was angry about it.

What telegram?

The one he got yesterday night.

Weren't you there?

Yes. But wasn't I talking to someone?

Well, were you?

I guess I was.

Well, it was about—

It was from Toots.

Did you read it?

No, he read it out loud.

What did he say.

He was angry.

Must have been surprised, rather.

Yes, I guess so.

He doesn't love me.

It's no good, Kenneth said, the grass is impossible. I'm going to take a nap wake me for supper.

Phillip said Carolyn, you're marvelous, at supper.

What's the insignia on your hat.

I was at a camp an interracial camp when I was a kid, said Carolyn.

Counselor?

More or less.

The girls cleaned off the table and brought coffee.

This coffee is terrific.

Do you think anything's in the water?

They tell that scorpions take to the water in midsummer.

Oh cut it out.

Carolyn stood up and Peter took hold of a belt loop on her pants.

Where are you going.

I

Don't go, he said, standing up.

When she sat down Kenneth was reading from one of Peter's books.

Marvelous.

Listen to this.

She stood up and he took her wrist.

Stay a little.

I have to go.

Where.

Do the dishes.

In a half hour.

I have to, I want to read.

What, what?

Omoo.

In the morning Carolyn was the first one up.

Wake up wake up wake up wake up she sang going around.

I dreamed I saw you Carolyn, said Phillip.

I saw your face and it gleamed like tin, like polished tin. I saw two queens, in their robes, perfumed, splendid. One was the queen of Fact and the other of Fiction.

This is the Truth I said, and I pointed to the queen of Fact, because I know truth. I could tell Fact from Fiction because of the difference. Somehow they were apart. But they posed like one.

This is truth because truth declares the difference.

This is fiction because fiction cares not for distinction, cares only for face.

But what is truth, even an angel, to know, if it turns fiction, is unable to name its own face?

And then, once I know this what am I to say?

I had a dream last night, said Carolyn. I was standing by the road and three kings came by. One was the king of Gift and the other was the king of Take. The king of Gift was smiling and multitudes were strewing flowers about his feet. The king of Take was beating his temples, cursing the moment. The king of Gift was clothed in rags and the king of Take was of metropolitan dress. I ran out as they passed.

The king of Gift came to me, worshipped me. I kissed him fondly.

Then came the king of Take. Dogs and lechers were on his heels, beating their temples and cursing the moment.

Who is to take when there is nothing but gift? said the king of Take.

Then came the king of Both who passed by quietly, pensive.

A car passed them and, as it went up the slope of the road, behind them, in the other lane, the lights of a car, coming over the hill, increased brightly, as it proceeded. The car in the other lane rose to the peak of the hill as it went, the approaching car came closer and the disappearing car dimmed its front lights—its rear lights turned blue, the white lights of the other car, came over the hill at once.

There was a man who was lost in the desert. He was dying of thirst. He fell to his knees and crawled along. He crawled to the crest of a dune. Finally he reached the crest. Then he was over. On the other side of the dune was a huge building. He went inside. There was a huge hall with tremendous crystal chandeliers and a marble floor. As he came into the entrance way of this palace, in the huge hall, he saw many men stationed at chopping blocks, meat cutters' blocks, and they all were chopping pieces of meat. He struggled over to one and said to the man I'm dying of thirst. Can you tell me where I can get some water.

The man paid no attention. He went to another meat cutter.

Can't you see I'm dying of thirst. Can you—

but he saw the man wasn't listening. Then his curiosity got the best of him.

He looked around him at the men cutting meat. He went over to another cutter and pulled his apron.

Say, what are all you men doing I mean why are you—what are you doing?

The cutter turned to him and said

What's the matter with you? Can't you see we're jamming?

HIGH AND HIGH SPADE

AND WHAT *do* you think Christianity is? Do you think it is a composition of a few scattered meaningless totems, strewn about in primitive disorder? Do you think we live in a society such as that of an Australian bush beater?

No sir, I don't. I don't know what Christianity is, sir.

Well, you'd better find out. Tell me about Christ.

I can't sir.

But *why* can't you! Do you attribute your ignorance to some incomprehensible psychological trait achieved early in childhood that makes you invulnerable to such immediate questions, or do you really not know. Don't you know that He was born, that Christmas day is the day of celebration of Christ's birth? Do you know what Good Friday is? Do you know what Easter is?

Yes sir.

Sir. It's time sir. Hadn't we better go in?

Yes. Now when we enter, keep still. And when the Bishop speaks, listen closely. He has great intellect and great spirit. The first thing to—

You may come in now, said a little man wearing a light gray suit, stepping out of the door for a moment, and then going back in, saying that the Bishop was ready.

They went to their appointed row of folding chairs and sat down. There was an announcement made that there was a prayer in order and the slight talking stopped while everyone knelt and prayed. Then they sat back in their chairs and the quiet conversation resumed. The Bishop entered stage right and the talking stopped. The Bishop walked to the chair in front of the room, stood by it for a moment, smiled at everyone, and sat down and crossed one leg over the other.

THE ADDRESS:

My wife told me this morning that our clock, which is just above the sink in the kitchen, was broken, and that, with reference to the fact that our other clock in the bedroom had been broken three days ago, that was too much.

There was immediate necessity to get the clock repaired.

Both my wife and I have numerous appointments to keep during the day.

"Yes," I told her, "we shall have to get them fixed. It is too much not to know what the time of day is."

Now that is my point.

We all live in distinct time *zones*.

Just as there are layers of rock, there are layers of time.

When my wife told me about the clocks, I thought to myself, how is it that this particular event should take place just now when I have been so concerned with this lately, and of what uselessness is the clock! If I have my love of Christ, what necessity for the clock have I, when I have the time of the greatest Man to have yet lived?

You see, there is a time of Christ.

The time of Christ is your time.

If anyone should ask you what the time of day is, you answer,

It's Christtime.

If you hold Christ the master of all life, and God as the eternal Master of the master, and if you identify the life you have with the life of Christ and God, it is a life of correct direction

(30)

then. Your life, the time of your life is the time of Jesus. If it is not then, there is a terrible timeless death that you will die. Already you know of death. Each of us dies a thousand times a day. Then you know that a timeless death is absence of reality. Live the time of day with Jesus. He is there with you, to communicate with.

The time *zone* of Jesus is what you must involve yourself with. In Him there is a great hugeness. In Him there is a great unlimited boundary of rock layers and you must consider yourself bound to the grain of those rocks, because that strata is the strength in which He lived and died for you, so that, so your lives may have full meaning, have His meaning, in order for you to have *your* own life, so that you can have your *own* time at the same time that you are in the center of Christ Himself, so that the time will always be Christtime.

A DISCUSSION OF THE ADDRESS:

Clarence! What do you receive from his address.

I thought it was all right, sir. I thought the idea of Christtime was all right, sir.

Sir? Mister Alexander? Sir, William Faulkner says that watches are unnecessary!

That is correct, James. He also hints that Christ was a Negro.

Yes sir, in *Light in August*. And "Light" in *Light in August* means that a woman is pregnant in August.

That is true, Arnold, but we must not stray too far away from the Bishop's address. William Faulkner is a fine writer, aside from the fact that his sentences are a little confusing, and he poses many interesting situations in his novels, but I don't think that he is completely in order here.

Do you think, sir, if you'll pardon me, that Christ could have been a Negro?

No, I don't think so. I think that the reason for Faulkner using a Negro as he did, to mean Christ, was because he sets himself in a limited area, in his novels, and writing about the particular kind of people he does write about, it is natural to assume that if he would choose to write about Christ, that he would pick a Negro for the role. The same in *The Wild Palms*, Harold, where he projects a kind of Odyssey in The Old Man, as against the civilized society of *The Wild Palms*.

Why, sir.

Yes sir, why not a White man?

Well, I don't think that Faulkner believes that the White Man has the kind of History, or myth, that the Negro does, that the Negro of African origin some thousands of years ago would have the similar capacity for legend or myth or force in any given time, that Christ Himself would have, in His time, coming out, as he did, then.

I don't understand, sir.

He means that the Negro in *Light in August* and The Old Man is the only figure capable of Christ now, just as Christ Himself was capable of himself then. Is that right, sir?

Yes. Now . . . in what way does what we are talking about now have relevance to the address that the Bishop has just given?

Sir?

One at a time, Louis. Now—what?

That even the time of William Faulkner is the time of Christ.

Yes Louis, very good.

But why does Faulkner say that watches are useless, then. He says that in a different environment, a different context than what we are discussing, don't you think so sir?

(32)

I don't know what book you're referring to, but I'm sure that the situation is different.

It's *Sound and Fury*, sir.

Oh yes. Well, I haven't read it.

I believe in Christ, sir, and I believe that any time even now is when Christ can help us.

Yes sir, so do I.

That's true Dorothy, Jimmy, but I think that there is a deeper meaning just the same, that the Bishop was talking about, and this is what I want you to understand. Here is what I propose to do. We are going to have a little off the cuff play, here, now, and the first thing I want you to do is to choose a moment in the life of Christ that will be most meaningful in terms of what the Bishop said. Harold?

The Last Supper.

I don't think so. Dorothy?

Christmas.

Nooo. Louis?

When John baptizes Him.

Maybe—we'll consider that one. I have one moment in mind, however, that I think will be fine. Arnold?

The Sermon on the Mount, sir?

Excellent, Arnold, we will do the Sermon on the Mount.

(ALL:) YOU, SIR! YOU BE CHRIST!

(He blushes slightly) I shall be Christ.

THE PLAY, CONCERNING CHRIST AND HIS SERMON ON THE MOUNTAIN:

Cast
JESUS: The Savior. Mr. Alexander
MARY: The mother of Jesus. Dorothy

MOOR: Moor of Egypt. Clarence
WISE MAN: Wise Man from Jerusalem. Harold
LEPER: Leper of Jerusalem
MULTITUDE AND VOICES: From the surrounding territory.

Christ stands now, and looks at the vast crowd of people before Him. It is a fine day, the powder blue sky is unusually high and the long green grass of the mountainside bends to the delicate push of the breeze. He stands for a moment, pensive, and then, raising His arms, He speaks.

CHRIST: I. . .

LEPER: Take off thy mask. Thou art a woman.

WISE MAN *(aside)*: Not even a woman.

MARY: What? What?

MOOR: It is a plot unconceived insofar as this has never happened and, furthermore, in all probability, will not happen at all unless, perhaps, the characters change with the plot, and, as we all know, that is rare—much too much so because such progression of our actions goes often to the contrary of ourselves, eliminating the probability of logical actions, which is what is happening before your very eyes, and in conclusion, no one else understands what is taking place on this mountain, much less you, son, and much less myself.

VOICES: CHRIST SPEAK CHRIST!

CHRIST: I . . .

LEPER: THE MASK THE MASK!

> *(Jesus removes the mask. It is true. He is a woman. She stands looking at the multitude from the top of the mountain. In her right hand is the false face of Christ.)*

WISE MAN: How now! A change of face.

MOOR: Who Mary—which?

MARY: Neither.

(34)

LEPER *(runs to the top of the mountain)*: I AM THE I AM THE CHRIST: FOOL FOOL IDIOTIC CLOD TO MY TIME.

WISE MAN: If it *is* so, then take off the second face.

CHRIST: I shall.

(Jesus holds her right arm to the multitude, and she takes off her mask with her left.

It is neither the face of a man nor a woman, but of a Jackal. The Jackal speaks.)

JACKAL: Now the event is of a different nature, is it not? It is a plurality of identities, and I, who regard you as *number,* deliver word from the singular.

(Turns to the Leper)

Off Leper. Remove thy mask.

(The Jackal tears at the Leper's face for the mask. There is no mask.)

MARY: It is too much. I leave.

MOOR: Wait! Wait! *(Exit together)*

(The Jackal goes away down the mountain, shaking his head, weeping.

The Wise Man moves into the multitude. He speaks.)

WISE MAN: It is not I who moves like this. It is another thing. I am out, with Mary and the Moor. Things are of a different order at this instant. It is an unwise step I take. Ugh, how they push—hark! He speaks!

Curtain

(35)

SALAD

SHE SAT AT THE LUNCH TABLE. It was a remarkable day, I thought, because the sun kept going dark and bright because of the sudden clouds that would obscure it at one moment and then it would be blazing white again. They had a nice cottage. It was a summer cottage on the river, with a small leaky rowboat that they went rowing in, in the evenings. They thought that fine fun, she told me, going out like that, in the evening, in that boat. He called it The Essex, and he told me how they had both laughed when he got out his paint and lettered on the stern, "THE ESSEX," as she stood watching him, sitting on the bank, watching him paint.

He sat next to her smiling like that, like he smiled after he finished painting the name on the stern of the rowboat, standing up and saying, holding the brush in his hand saying,

Now, how's that, I say!

I say that's fine, she said, and then he smiled.

She was wearing a light blue jumper with a white blouse on beneath and very pretty, her blond hair kept clean, kept right, like at school, at the university. And she served the food just right, pouring the milk from the heavy blue and white china pitcher, standing up and pouring.

The river, he explained, was down a little because it had not rained for a while, and it was fairly clear, but, when it rained, the river would muddy up some.

It was not a very large river, not very wide, not deep. But it was pleasant in the summer.

In front of the cottage it was not very nice though, because of the highway. The highway ran in front of the cottage. She told me before lunch as we looked at the river that she didn't like the highway there.

No, she said, I don't like it. You know, I don't like the highway there at all.

Now she was proud, walking along, down the path with me, as I was between the two, herself and him, and she looked at the river as we went along, walking between the slope and the river, on the path, and she smiled grimly because when she was proud, that was how she was, grim.

The slope was not very high, higher than we were, but not high in that it formed a cliff or something such, but only up a slight height, being a stiff grade, almost sheer, to the highway, which ran parallel to us, as we walked.

Up ahead was the cottage, small, two stories, green and white, built on high struts for flood season, almost every year, late in the summer when the river rose, went over the banks, onto the highway. Every year someone was killed. A house would wash away.

It was something to see. The houses standing up, all colored green and white, brown and white, blue and white, or another, and the trees sticking up in the muddy water, in calmly shifting currents, losing, regaining force.

Look, she said, pointing across the river, there is a little boy swimming. I just saw him dive from the pier. Now wait till he comes out—wait now.

But what does he know, he said.

How to swim, she said—and dive—see? God, isn't that something. All dive, no talent.

A car went by above us.

We walked up the steps of the cottage. They were wooden

and dusty from the dried mud of the river and they went to the side of the house, directly, then turned, following the wall of the house, to the screen door of the porch.

God, she said, what a day! Isn't it something!

You know, she said, when I was little, in Illinois, we lived near a big creek and when it rained we would lie on our stomachs on the bridge and hang pieces of rope into the current and drag out pieces of driftwood, for the fire, when winter came. On days like this, though, we would sit on the porch and look at the trees. Sometimes the spiders, those Daddy-long-leg spiders, would be so thick on the screens, we couldn't see out. They would be in our beds at night, on our table at mealtimes, everywhere, and I never minded them. I saw one one day and it had a broken leg, their legs are so long, and the way it was shattered me. And when we picked flowers and put them in the vase on the table, they would go up the side of the vase and look in, and then climb up and sit on the bloom of the flower. I'd kill for that. Kill and kill and kill for that.

They sat on the swing on the front porch, and I sat in a wicker chair. It was dark and the insects buzzed now and then, as they collided with the screen. It was very dark outside, and a slight breeze was blowing. When the breeze died, though, everything was quite still, save for the accidental sounds of the insects, bumping into the screen. The light in the living-room was on, behind us, and I guess it was that that they were trying to get to. I rather enjoyed the quietness. When cars went by, now and then, they were only heard because we could see their headlights as they came by. But the weight of the dark, even with the breeze, clamped echo. It made silences between words pronounced, distinct.

(38)

How often do the buses run, I said.
Every hour.
Well, I said, it's nine now. At ten, I'll go.
The nine bus went by then. I turned and looked at them.
That's racket, she said.

THE SUN RISES INTO THE SKY

.

REMEMBER PEARL HARBOR

For Ed & Jennifer

SHE OPENED THE DOOR of the refrigerator and took out the lettuce; she took out the mayonaise; she took out the butter and milk, and she closed the door and took out the peanut butter from the cupboard and after taking the breadloaf from the breadbox, she made a peanut butter sandwich he would like, and eating it and drinking the glass of milk she looked out the window.

The lawn sloped like a long backyard to the neighbor's backyard; they were forever sitting in their backyard; her little hedge hadn't done much good, and she looked at her sloping backyard lawn a nice lawn and she looked into the living room where no television set stood.

Her husband sat on that sofa every Sunday and read *The Post-Dispatch;* she missed him there.

Out of the corner of her eye a figure—at ease in a humorous way—stood on the lawn, and as she smiled and turned, realized no one was there. She looked in again where her husband would be if it were Sunday and saw the figure out of her eye on the lawn. It looked like, smiling as the man was, curiously, like Gatsby.

Her son lay beside a beautiful captain's wife on the beach in Hawaii, and they necked; her son felt he had made a conquest, it surely was a form of something that he could go in and out of Headquarters Gates with her driving her car, and then, having her there, must be something, too, yet, he postulated, if she wasn't a captain's wife it wouldn't mean what it did, she would be what she was without being a captain's wife and he would

(43)

be a guy.

In the mind of the man on the beach beside the other man's wife she and he strode differently; what was extraordinary about it they were their own experience as well away as at home; misunderstanding was across the water.

Boyishly he grinned: "Let the rest of the world—"

"Yeah," she murmured. "Go by. I believe."

"What's the matter?" he asked.

She looked at him. She didn't love him, but she loved to fuck with him, and she turned to him, and confusing him, said,

"Hold me."

He held her and gazed at the Pacific.

The man just stood there, smiling. Where had he come from? She munched the sandwich, wondering.

The sunlight streamed as if forever, through the windows as they rose and fell, like sex in a slick magazine he wondered about her intense pleasure, and not like a hammer; she was purely delighted, and the man, the other man, who flew hundreds of miles away thought of her in the sky, of her face. How he yearned to love her! He would take her to the dance this weekend, and blinding lines crossed his face, and the enemy planes were by them even as he wheeled, wheeling looking at them and the holes their 30 caliber bullets had made in the cockpit. He saw his were four, and theirs were six.

She was gone as he worked the machinegun on its pivot, and yelled over his shoulder to the pilot, "Get 'em Charley!" yet seeing the ships below.

"*You* get 'em," Charley snapped back, and he moved around seeing the Zeroes coming in just under the sun, and firing, looping his heavy 50s out watching the enemy planes' wing guns spit lines at him he saw his shells strike and strike again, the belly of the enemy plane zoomed over, another, and Charley banked and 30 caliber shells tore through the housing, and he saw the third Zero had them—

Charley yelled—"Heads up!"

Frantically, furiously he swiveled his guns as the plane banked, and suddenly dived, the Zero was out of sight and then he saw it zip underneath, but underneath was up above, and the enemy plane twinkled away, his plane levelled, the sea and sky and clouds fell into place and he saw two Zeroes come in like ten to twelve, towards him, the sky was so bright behind their approaching crisscross he sighted under them firing above, looping a crazy lateral figure 8 clothesline of bullets and as Charley dove very fast to the right the Zero coming in on 12 blew up, and the plane on ten to was beyond them so close overhead, and so quickly gone he only realized he was in a panic crouch fighting with the guns to get them around pointlessly because one plane was down and the other was gone by, and he remembered him and Charley yelling "There's one! There's one!" hysterically, the housing smashed and shredded from shells, and his skin crawling with fear, and the Zeroes hung on, rising and coming at them again, riddling the torpedo planes, yet the torpedo planes hung on, too, and went in low, into the meat of the broadside destroyer fire, Charley letting the torpedo go while the Zeroes chased them from above, while the inverted gull-winged Grummans chased the Zeroes, the man at the guns doing his part altogether angrily, there wasn't anything else to do, and there they were, and so he fired at at them, and saying hey Charley, and the old plane for some reason was all by itself over the Pacific, and the ships and fighters way behind, Charley, and then he saw a torpedo plane to his right, climbing, and then another was on its way up, too, and he said, "Hey, Charley," and twisted around in the wreckage, "What happened?" Charley didn't know, Charley had been hit.

"Can you make it in?"

Charley hated him. Boy did he hate him. And Charley made it in. He was afraid of Charley, even with the planes—the Zeroes, the destroyers, the cruisers—firing at him—what he was really afraid of was Charley; he sat at the table, looking a little haunted as she made coffee, and when she served it to him, her hands trembled.

THE STORY

THE WIND TORE THROUGH the snow covered suburbs as I faced
her, stammering I knew the artist who had drawn the Christmas card on her mantlepiece, and I pointed to the one card out
of dozens; what I said apparently didn't register.

She was five feet six squat with a drowsy voice and a squall-
ing baby at her heels, her husband was in the room down the
hall she said, getting dressed. "To go nowhere," she said.

Behind my back the suburbs slanted, like hopscotch, over
and beyond every city, towards the plains and infinity; cold and
barren—I said I didn't mean to be a name-dropper that, seeing
his drawing I knew him; I had studied with—well, I said that
the Museum of Modern Art must have asked him—a man's
voice from down the hallway asked something—

I always saw him in the sky in the stories he never told me,
of the gunner he was, in action in his torpedo plane, and I
could see it go in, just a few feet above the water heading into
all hell of fire dropping the torpedo and sweeping upward in a
prayer to get away alive, and the nausea he must have felt as
they did make it. He was a nice looking guy, to me.

He shook my hand, I was at school remembering how he
came home, and she picked up her baby and nuzzled it—face to
face—and the hair on my neck began to crawl, I was out of
college, suddenly, and they were moving in a dream of slowly
moving animals advancing on their shadows stretching out
across the plain, ahead of them, and with the sun behind her,
she gazed upon me, gazing as a sheep upon me, a sullen dense

animal stare as he came into the room fixing a cufflink and then shaking my hand, grinning it's nice to see you—in the absence of enemy fire his face, later, singing Christmas carols at the piano in and by the pine smell fireplace, in my house, he had a funny split pink look, one eye reading the lyrics and the other trying to see out of the back of his head, get the guns trained on her, and let her have it, as she sat by the fire, smiling, drinking punch, talking with somebody out of the past, as he squeezed the trigger, snarled,

"Nowhere, eh?"

Cocked his eye on the Virgin's womb.

THE GIRL ON THE BICYCLE
(A Mystery)

for Marge

THE SUBURBAN WIFE is to my right on the studio couch and we are talking; it is a late blue afternoon in October. Diaphragms swell as we talk—"Do you believe in God?" she asks me, holding Mozart in her left hand.

It was a long time ago. I looked at a man in a blue cord suit who was talking to his friend's wife, and noticing his profile intent upon her I saw it was nothing like mine, and in New York the great poet sat on my shoulder and snarled, "How wise! Wise! How *wise* you are!"

"Yes," I grinned, and her face smoothed falling, asked, "I asked: God, not an idea: do you believe in God?"

I said I did, not in, but I said I believed God and I shook my head in vertical force and she looked at me laterally. Secretly smiled.

It was the second time I had seen her; the first had been a few years before when my brother-in-law and my sister had taken me—the bright sixteen year old younger brother—to a movie and afterwards to meet some very interesting people, we rang the bell I yet hear her distant call which emitted a laugh of fright because someone was ringing the bell at that crazy hour, and a smile because maybe somebody was calling on her? and an error which kept the smiling laughing possibility of someone apart from her—no matter what loving music he would make, no one would ever come to her, and we went in I, I rifled a little affection to her—she said excitedly, she was really glad to see us! My sister introduced me, and her husband shook my hand, he was a tall and handsome man whom I liked

as I would have liked myself had I known; so we sat and drank
coffee and she in her vivid bid, a double pitch forward to be it
and also represent—be seen as—laughed and bubbled and her
husband likewise although a little coolly we had a great time,
and eight years later a question of God in the second meeting
on a sunfilled porch of the October month at someone's house,
on a porch in the suburbs soft music flowed out over the yard
and the elderly couple shopkeeper and wife were drunk and I
matched a few drinks with him while his wife danced alone in
the living room and I caulking my brain dome loving the
woman on the porch towards our third and so, to our fourth
meeting—fifth and sixth and sexual embraces a long story of
art and children, deception and desire and psycho-analysis, and
Jung, and Mozart, and religion with a woman who youthfully
turns into age without herself, I see her lined face and that
soft, that great soft complicated defensive laugh she has under
her male grin, she should be among women creatures, on the
island away from her stories, and away from our love, and the
thunder of our God; each time she appeared to me she came
with the enthusiasm of discovery she came to me with a hope I
would turn her into her and I failed I took her into my arms;
she came to me, the girl I know, searching for me, leading me
to herself riding her bicycle up the driveway to my studio: her
moving figure in sweater and slacks anxious to encounter that
which she sees in me, better found in a tall woman, in blue adoration like October, and Mozart, God she asked me as in I held
His hand, yes I said, not in, yes I believe God, why sure, and.
And O Little Town of Bethlehem roared out of the house; I
scowled I looked across the porch of people at my sister appearing late there with her husband, sentimental about Christmas
Jesus unification of October all things into Oneness, a shriek
split the anachronistic mood, I went into the living room, the
shopkeeper's wife had a stack of long playing records in her

(50)

hands trying to break them over her knee threw them at me and ground as a stick in mud the needle on the Christmas carol tears running down her lined face turning paralyzed in hate her old tongue spitting through teeth God she snarled, God: *what*, she lunged at her husband—lunged by me into his arms with my own hands out; he soothed her as she wept stop—stop this is a lie. The doctor's wife did grind the needle into the record, but when I came into the room she became hysterical because I was startled, she laughed she mocked me; jumping; jumping by me, my outstretched hands; why did I invent her husband soothing her?

She stands in my mind, I see her face. I tried to write her in action but her action is not her identity and she is an aged and ungainly creature from where I start towards her, toward the complication of my mother and my feminine surrounded childhood, of my age and maleness, I thought she should react to that, so I wrote that she threw the records at me, I had her jump—by my godly outstretched hands, into the comfort of her husband's, and I am and am not, and in truth she mocked me. She stood by the bookcase and record player sending waves of her emotion toward me, waves of my life, the great strange waves from earliest childhood, in her.

—I didn't believe her face was its image of her, her face rode a neck above a moving torso, and what I saw was mine—I rushed into the room and saw the witchness mocking and laughing in the center of memories and identities, found a face so ordinarily ghastly I could give it to question God and throw things, that it would come from the beginning and live as we live, yet from its origin in the waves her face came up the driveway to me as I would come to myself, with all the charm, intelligence and adoration of me I so oddly understand, and did encounter that October afternoon.

Strange love.

THE HIGHWAY CHAIR

For Dr. Pearlman

*As I left she came close to me in the
doorway: "I'm not perceptive like you
are! I can't say things like you can!
But I know! I know!"*

IN THE FLATIRON BUILDING

I was talking with my dentist and his assistant a slender
blonde girl with blue-grey eyes, she was sensitive she was
nervous she was keeping things to herself.

Doctor Back was an active Naval Reserve officer a power-
fully built city man in his middle thirties with a sense of duty
and order yet he punished himself, he was self-conscious and
he was lonely. I sat in the dental chair I went on:

"I had been out of the Army only a few weeks and one night
I was going drunkenly from one bar to another and ended up
in a place on Highway 66. I had one drink and left.

"The doorway had the effect of a side door, but was sheltered
outside by a lattice construction. I stepped out as a man brush-
ed by: my dentist from childhood, his face flashed darkly by
me, he went in the bar quickly, a woman came up the sloping
grass after him, rage and bitterness on her face."

Doctor Back was talking about his mother in Brooklyn he
was going there for supper tonight he shaped the cap for my
tooth I looked out the window at buildings across Fifth Avenue.

"Well well well! Mister Wax!"

The doctor had snickered. I glanced at him. He looked back at me, eyes twinkling, exclaiming tinnily nastily "Mister Wax!"

"Mister Wax is our *dental salesman,* and even though we don't need anything we make an order don't we Betty." Doctor Back sprang to his supply cabinet opening and closing doors and drawers calling code numbers and names of powders fluids metals Mister Wax made notations murmuring yes, all right, fine Doctor Back looked at me "I want you to meet our dental salesman Mister Wax, Mister Wax has been coming to us for––" Mister Wax stood against the wall Doctor Back faced: "Mister Wax has been coming to us for *seven years* seven Mister Wax?"

Mister Wax smiled. "Seven years."

I turned in the chair to look back at Mister Wax middle aged transient worn balding distracted smiling face lined by a lifetime in this city that city pointed to a Cinzano ashtray

"Pretty interesting looking ashtray, where'd you get it?"

Doctor Back cried: "Mister Wax! The ashtray is yours! Betty wrap up the ashtray I got in Paris and give it to Mister Wax! Mister Wax ask, and you shall receive! Betty wrap it up, that's right, take it in the office, there's some paper and a bag in the desk. Mister Wax gets his ashtray!" Doctor Back snapped his fingers "Mister Wax! How about bringing some clean towels next Monday. What we need is some clean towels."

Mister Wax mumbled. "I don't know I'll try, Doctor, but I'm not sure I can get 'em to you next Monday. I'd be—"

"Oh any time! No hurry!"

Mister Wax laughed "I'd be a liar if I promised I'd have 'em here by next Monday."

Doctor Back said vehemently: "There is no rush, Mister Wax."

Betty gave Mister Wax the bag with the ashtray enclosed and stood by the window. Doctor Back glared at Mister Wax:

"Anything else—speak up Mister Wax! Ask and you shall receive!"

Mister Wax grinned "How about giving me Betty?"

Doctor Back's hands exploded in a single clap. "Betty! You are as of this moment fired! You will go with Mister Wax. Mister Wax, Betty is yours!"

I jumped from the dental chair.

Mr. Wax looked at Doctor Back. "Naw. I was just kiddin'."

"Yes!" I said, "It was the Doctor's joke. Don't go Betty!"

Doctor Back snarled *"Joke!* Betty: go with Mister Wax!"

I pointed: I harshly said: "Betty isn't going with Mr. Wax. Why would Betty want to go with Mister Wax? Mister Wax doesn't want Betty—and Betty doesn't want Mister Wax and I don't want Betty to go with Mister Wax!" Mister Wax moved toward the door Doctor Back panting watched him and Betty watched me. I watched Doctor Back, Mister Wax left the room went into the reception office, went into the waiting room, the door into the hall closed and Mister Wax was gone Doctor Back said, "I can't go back on my word. Anything Mister Wax wants he gets and he said he wanted Betty."

I sat down shaking my head "No! Mister Wax asked you quote How about giving me Betty unquote, why didn't he ask her? Because of you, as if she wants to go with Mister Wax: who made it clear he was just kidding."

Doctor Back said, "I can't go back on my word."

"Why not?"

Doctor Back sang softly "When I say something I can't go back on it."

I said angrily, "It's yours!"

"I can't."

Doctor Back sat on the stool by the dental chair, sanded and airhosed the cavity of the cap and fitted it on my tooth. "Bite down."

I asked, "Why didn't you hit him? You wanted to."

The Doctor's eyes blazed that desire: I said "Stay away from your mother in Brooklyn tonight; go to Mister Wax. Hit him."

MAN STEPS INTO SPACE

For Martha

AFTER WORK the big blonde salesgirl from Texas sat on a bar-stool beside Thomas; he had gone to the bank to make the evening deposit and she had crossed the avenue gone into the bar and ordered two large steins of Ballantine, and as he entered she pulled the stool out and he joined her, both murmuring hello hello to each other touching the steins hoisting and drinking.

It was seven o'clock on a hot summer evening New York girls had come from work eaten washed up and were walking with friends to and from the department stores and Thomas and the salesgirl from Texas talked and Thomas watched the parade as evening turned into night a particularly pretty girl passed, and for a moment looked Thomas's way. The charm of her face and sweetness of flesh in summer clothes touched him, and yet took him into another consciousness, she disappeared in the crowd and he was puzzled; the blonde salesgirl watched a slow frown darken his face and she loved him because he was funny and brilliant; they supplemented each other's need for friendship side by side selling furniture everyday and week and when she saw the pretty girl look at Thomas Thomas double-crossed the girl from Texas by going into his mind and closing the door. Okay; she winked.

"What is it?" she asked. "I saw her."

Thomas looked at her and shook his head.

She said bitterly, "You're real fun."

He nodded and moved his hands as if searching through smoke, "I hear voices," he said and she nodded, "You're crazy."

(56)

"Yes," he nodded; he told her a different story.

She was disgusted; his story, she thought, didn't have that much in it, Thomas looked at her and said, "It does and it doesn't, depending on where you're sitting," and he smiling flicked the switch: sitting.

Sound of laughter.

It was yellow face again, sitting to his left as the girl appeared—and as Thomas was startled by the masked figure in the corner of his eye the girl went away in the crowd Thomas's heart yet following—cherry lips in yellow said,

"Put her face before your eyes."

Thomas did so, and as red lips opened and closed Thomas nodded in a comprehension of grief and loneliness, and the harlequin man, the fellow with the yellow face and blue plume of hair gazed sternly at him.

Surely, behind her pretty face I did see misery of loneliness and an unknown despair of existence and I knew her attractive body would not be resiliant; that she would be in fact vague in all ways. You are right. Her eyes were fearful and I saw their deep dullness; the dull smokecenter covering what she was afraid to be. Red lips moved again.

Look—but then let her go by! Lean toward the wife whom you fear—who is different from you. And what is a pretty face, and a body seeming in summer clothes? The wrong dream, only you lead you to your own art, where your face is, she is; do you see you, my Thomas? Yellow laughed a savage amusement. Why don't you be me? I'm not afraid of your wife.

Around a year later Thomas had a dream.

He was walking down that avenue; the rain had stopped, bright colors of neon signs reflected off cars, wet asphalt and glass windows; the air was fresh, sharp and though it was summer he was chilled, although warm as if his wife were within him—he sensed his friend the blonde Texan girl near him in a knowing way and his feet were bare.

He pushed open the swinging doors of the tavern and went in but the bar was old in a different way, a hollow way, and Thomas stood in his feet tracks on the floor saying to the owner, "Where's the familiar bartender Ireland?"

"Ireland doesn't work here anymore," the owner gravely said. Thomas frowned and experienced sorrow. He turned, and the food counter, which had been just inside the door, was without the usual refrigerator and stove, and pots and pans— "Where's Pop?" Thomas asked. The owner shook his head, his rimless glasses glinted sharp: "Gone," he said, and Thomas trudged up and down the wet avenue looking in and out of stores for his shoes.

That was the year Thomas quit selling furniture, he got a new job working with an importing firm and one day he sat at his desk by the window on the sixteenth floor looking out at the city with the telephone in his hand, he was dialing the number of the old furniture store, sitting tipped back in the swivel chair running his eyes up and down the Empire State Building; the switchboard operator's voice said the name of the furniture store, Thomas said um hum and asked for the uptown branch and the operator fondly said hello to him. He grinned across the city to her; "Hi sweetheart; how are you?"

"Fine," she smiled, and he saw her face before him. She paused—"How are you?"

"Fine. I have a new job—are you looking?"

"Yes I heard—not yet," she laughed, "though I ought to be." Then she said softly, "This dump."

Thomas chuckled, "Amen."

"Here's uptown," she said, and the big blonde girl—Texas voice said the name of the store—"Uptown." Thomas said hello.

She cried "Oh God, how I miss you!"

After work he took the BMT uptown and met her as the furniture store closed, they crossed the avenue pushing open swinging doors to two large steins of Ballantine at the bar, toasted and drank and lit cigarettes; the owner smiled and asked Thomas if he had a new job, yes, how was it, fine, and Ireland came on duty pulling his white apron around by the string and tying it across his waist while he treated himself to a shot of Scotch with icewater chaser and inquired if Thomas had a new job yes—pay better? Sure, Ah, and the health of the blonde from Texas—while at the same moment a different figure with flat cheeks and thin lips sitting beside Thomas leaned and touched shoulders with him saying out of the corner of his undertone imitating a shadow a thumb appearing by Thomas's cheek the figure pressed close, "Did ya notice?" Thomas looked where the thumb pointed—the food counter was without the usual refrigerator and stove, pots and pans, "I had a dream," Thomas said, his eyes on those eyes of the figure which darkened in cynicism; thin lips moved, "Whaddya mean a dream—" "I mean a dream," Thomas said, "the food counter was closed." The figure nodded bitterly and Thomas turned to the blonde girl: "I had a dream."

"A dream," she smiled. "Thomas Crimmins had a dream."

He told her the dream. "Okay," she said, "and thanks." He told her to look, she did, she didn't get it. Look carefully, he said: the refrigerator, the old stove and all the banged up pots and pans old Pop used were gone and so was Pop. She looked at Thomas carefully, and slowly a fine perception came into her eyes, she touched his hand, "Thomas Crimmins," she whispered; "you are fantastic."

THE PRIDE OF THE YANKEES

I GOT A LINE SINGLE to center which scored Mantle and sent Maris to third yet Dickey was waving me to take second. I had come in from center a little too fast, the ball hit my glove wrong, it bounced off my wrist and over my shoulder and went into center yet I had come across from left and covered as I came at the ball seeing me go into second, I picked the ball up with my webbing but of all things dropped it, I picked it up again and furiously fired it to second, my throw was to the third base side of the bag, but I caught it and pivoting with a kind of leap not to get spiked I slapped the glove across as I came in hard, knowing I was safe I made the traditional umpire gesture of safe which irritated me as I knew I had made the tag. I was wild in the stands. Maris had scored and as I came to bat I looked down to Yogi for the signal.

"Boy," Mantle later teased me, "it's lucky you goofed in center, you never would have made second."

THE DREAMER

THE DREAMER CROSSED 23rd St. and headed down Broadway, and out of the crowd a feminine body moved in front of him, a walking body so clear the dreamer focused anew; her legs were beautifully moulded in muscle, and her thighs, swinging under the cotton dress were weights in movement her buttocks were hard and her back broad and straight as a wall and her shoulders were square; long soft shining sun hair hung off her oval head to her shoulderblades.

Truckers and businessmen scattered before her, grinning and gazing, eyes wide in fear and awe, and dreaming Fielding knew to face her she would be a fine forward-moving ship to come towards; so he passed her, glancing to see her profile.

A golden profile of the finest shaped figure with breathtaking features. She was a solid woman in every way then, and his heart went to her; she was savagely beautiful.

The dreamer walked on, dazzled in love; he would kneel at her feet, double bases of bone and flesh for the living statue of speechless beauty and feminine power—yet no matter what he thought, his perception had told him the story, and what was then became now in her too clear eyes in his mind and as he walked he recalled the sensation he had had of lovely gray blue eyes—glass targets empty of emotion, and his heart sank to her for she sat in her head with her eyes shut as she sailed along without looking at all at the eyes that saw her and didn't see her at all; and the dreamer considered her history, a difficult life, he concluded. At 19th St., before he turned the corner, he glanced back.

She came down Broadway like a fine queen of a woman-ship, her free breasts so full, even under the loose dress half moon shadows cupped down, and her belly was so potently carved the wind against her made it seem a muscle moving in her powerful step, strong, firm, stepping feet carrying her onward—how utterly handsome she was! How ancient! High forehead, straight nose, sensitive serious strong mouth, her ears went flat against her head.

And her sun hair went straight back from her face, over the sleek crown of her oval head down her shoulders her moving shoulders squarely built for wide swinging arms: She, sweeping down Broadway.

She had a downward pointing crescent-moon mouth.

Her face spread from her ears when she laughed, nervously, without happiness, bubbling that I was talking to her, and her eyes darkened as she saw me saying something tensely funny, her pale eyes pressed back and her eyelids puffed, and as her eyebrows constricted because I was talking, there was perspiration on my forehead, in talking to her, and in a sudden anger her face was a terrible sight. Especially her mouth, amid furniture.

In a honey colored tweed suit, yellow shirt open at the collar with a yellow and green paisley silk scarf; tan gloves; fluffy brunette hair with streaks of blonde; eyes shallow under a forehead like a cliff. Her nose was straight, and she had perfect teeth. Her face was tan pancake.

Her hands trembled as she asked me, I anxious salesman in the uptown furniture store, if the glassware, on the shelf, there, was Swedish? No, I grinned, not at that price; very American, I said, "Say—34th Street?" But.

She was gone, and through the plate glass window I watched her walk down the chilly March avenue, mouth gnashing the wind.

He had gone to the party. It was the same house, yet a little —larger, or longer, and partly unfinished. There was a part that seemed longer. He walked along it—there were a lot of people and they greeted him, he greeted them he was happy yet a dark spot in his heart sent his eyes sharply on the faces.

All the faces.

Then, at his side, he was, greeting him in an old way, and turning to greet him he was already lost, and he reached for an old thing, like to take a going flower or moving leaf slanting everything all the guys and dolls in New York had said, he was gone and the top of the leaf was gone in the night out of reach.

Wandering down the wooden architectural places he saw his father with the silver glasses and they spoke coolly and warmly out of time.

DREAM DREAM Gone and all backs turned—brother, brother he asked how are you brother, he was well. But the brother was shy, and gray of face.

He turned away.

Down he followed him the metropolitan corridors "What will you do?" he cried, as a fist across, and he fell reeling, he asked, "What will you do?"

He chased him through Saint Louis—on all the dull street-cars and buses transferring at Maplewood and Clayton ahead of him,

"What will you do?"

—seized him on the lawn, the glassy music of the cocktail party coming out the windows—

And so he turned his back on him and left him. The remaining figure looked, longing, lonely; yet they were gone. All gone, dead, living, and gone. And looking into his father's grave on a wind they all moved away. The man with the silver glasses, the searched-for brothers, and the dreamer.

And with all the powers of heaven and hell as drunk as a man could ever be he walked the streets of New York, trying to figure it out he walked down toward the pavement and the upward motion of his mind.

BONAPARTE'S RETREAT

for Larry

IT WAS THE END OF APRIL. I was in a bar on 18th St. having a highball and dully reading *The Times* when a truckdriver came in, got a glass of beer, drank a sip, and abruptly turned to me.

"Hi," he said, with a big phony grin and a handshake he began talking about himself, he didn't want to bend my ear, he said, but he had been in the 2nd War, was a truckdriver now, and he was getting overtime, right now, and he poked the bar with his index finger: here, and though he had had, and had accepted, opportunities, many, with other women, the wife was the best, and he said he gave her his paycheck and she stayed at home—out on the Island—with his two kids, the girl, and the boy—the kid—but the kid was old enough to be in college because he—was, come to think of it, in, college, the wife didn't have to worry about that, and he had bought the kid a car for his birthday and a shotgun for Christmas, and the wife wouldn't have to worry—work, pardon him, again, because he had a good job with TEXACO driving the truck, he made a good salary, and he was a individual, had arranged his life so he could be a individual and live his life as he wanted with the wife and kids, but he missed the army, he had tried to re-enlist more than once but it was no go on account of the kids and he was forty-five. You're thirty-five?

I nodded.

He said he never hurt anybody except the enemy, and even then he was only doin' his duty obeyin' orders maybe them commies and pinkos would think he was pretty dumb and though he was a pretty liberal guy none of this commie shit was going to go by him he had seen listen, he said, I seen what them commies done to kids, babies, he underlined, in the Philippines, I can't go along with that never, he said, and pouted looking at me with his clever eyes.

Pinkos and commies would think he was crazy talking like he did, but he was really—look, he said, I'm only a guy with a job. I'm only doin' what I'm told to—

Orders, I said.

You got it, he said.

He said, they say deliver the oil here and there so I do it, right?

I asked, What was it like in the Philippines?

He stuck out his lower lip again and shook his head. Naw, he said. I was there. I only obeyed orders. Like you, right?

Not quite, I said; it's different, and his unhappy eyes narrowed watching me.

He grinned and horse's teeth split his face and said he was going to have one more and go home. The wife would be angry, he said. He didn't touch his beer. He named her the ball and chain.

He pointed a greasy finger at my face, and pulling an invisible trigger, said,

I'd blow your head off if you were my enemy, and I wouldn't think twice about it. But I wouldn't harm a hair on your head otherwise. Yeah, he continued:

I'm the kind of guy that says if nobody hurts me I don't hurt them, just let me drive my truck and let me alone to go home to my house out on the Island and you be you and I be me and my own. Right?

It's your way, I said, and finished my drink and ordered another, sliding the glass into the bartender's hand. The truckdriver was gulping his beer, he had to finish it, he did and anxiously gave it to the bartender asking for another. The glass —jumped into the bartender's hand.

I paid for my drink and sipped. The truckdriver likewise. He made a faint gesture and said, You know, I arranged my life. He said how much he missed the army but after he got out he was a Greyhound bus driver and he had had a lot of opportunities with other women and his eyes were soft and cruel as he had accepted the other women but none of them was as good, ever could be as the wife and he said when he got angry she sure did what he said. He looked at me and his eyes hardened. He grinned and looked away, said he was wonderful with kids, his daughter was nuts about him and when he came home at night, pulled the truck into the driveway there she was, waiting for him on the grass.

The kid's in college, he said, and didn't need his dad anymore because his boy was really on his own.

His voice rose. Only once, he got angry at his kids, his daughter bore a mark on her shoulder for days after; his eyes blazed over my head.

That must have shamed you, I said.

Yeah, he nodded, it was the only time, the one and one— only—he let the wife, take care of them in that way for from then on he gave his paycheck to her, the wife every week because money seemed to run through his fingers and once the wife's mother had defended him: why it's okay if he got drunk now and then, didn't he work all week for her and the kids? So he bought his wife a five hundred dollar mink coat for Christmas, you ought to see it! I sipped my drink.

He sipped his beer and said he was getting paid overtime and confided to me he missed the army because he preferred irresponsibility, he could put a gun in a man's face if it was a enemy and he was told to—them pinkos, the newspapers never told the truth, even not even about the niggers, why a white woman told him once a nigger spit in her face—boy, that wasn't in the papers! Then he said—

He said he wished he had married his wife's mother!

I laughed.

I got my whole life arranged, he said. His hands were out in front of him, fingers spread palms up. He said he was a truck-driver for TEXACO.

In the winter, he smiled. In the summer I drive a bulldozer. He glanced at my *Times*. It was folded showing the editorial page. He looked at me and it, and then at me, and frowned.

I only obey orders, he said. He chewed his lower lip. He asked me what my job was. I told him.

Part time job?

I nodded, and said I was a writer.

He tilted back in a big grin and said his kid had written a theme about the shotgun he'd bought him. His eyes were bright.

Then they were dark and irritated, the Goddamned teacher had written red marks all over his kid's theme! That God-damned teacher oughta be fired! he cried, didn't the neighbors agree with him? Yeah! They were big people, too, not just nobodies, top guys, *execs*, bigger than most!

I asked, What did the teacher write?

He said she wrote his kid couldn't write correct and his neighbor was an exec for IBM and the guy across the street was a chief in Howard Johnson and they read his kid's theme and thought it was pretty good!

I thought about executive hilarity as they read the TEXACO-man's son's theme, and as he said She marked it all up in *red*, I laughed outright, finished my drink, as he gave me a startled look, I picked up my paper, said goodnight, and walked outside still laughing; not looking back, you can be sure.

HEY THERE! ALL YOU PEOPLE

for Gil

DINAH WASHINGTON WAS SINGING,

"Funny thing,"

and the thick-necked woman said in a tough voice, to the very distracted man next to her, as she held her thumb aimed at the jukebox, "I knew a guy who knew her"; the man, his mustache in the center of his wide round face, mumbled, "Yeah?"

She nodded slowly, and said in italics: "He said she was really *something.*" She looked at the bartender who was watching her.

The round faced man mumbled, "Really something, eh?"

Her voice bit the word apart: "Some *thing,*" as if to the bartender.

The round faced man looked at her vaguely and nodded; the record stopped and Barbara Streisand began singing her people song and the woman said, with an invisible hand to one side of her mouth, her mouth, shaped like a diamond and top and bottom teeth stuck out like dice, in an undertone to the bartender,

"Just a Jew from Brooklyn." She looked at the man, and his mustache; she had droopy eyes. "But she's got talent, talent and no looks, it's her—she can sing is what I mean."

The man puffed on his cigarette and said, softly, "Yeah, she's good."

She gave the bartender a direct crooked smile; the bartender was wiping glasses and looking at her; he was a small slim forty-five year old Italian with haunted black eyes and his face

(69)

turned to the world, set, tightlipped, and a little bitter.

His gaze switched from her drawing power, and alarm waved through his eyes. "Cut it out Ellie," he said, and looked at her angrily.

"Why do you think it happened?" she asked him. She tossed it to him.

He put the glass on the bar and walked down the duckboards toward her, bunching the towel and standing in front of her, and cried, "Do you know how I feel now?"

"Yeah!" she yelled, standing and making a fist in front of his face and shaking it at him, spat, "And ditto for me!"

He flushed and swore at her and she swore at him, they shook their fists at each other, faces darkening, and then the little bartender pivoted and walked away. She as if appeared beside herself and asked him for a drink, he filled the shotglass with rye and gave her a glass of beer, took her money and rang it up without a word. He served another customer and began wiping glasses.

Then he looked at her; he said, softly, "You know, you remember; you knew then."

The velocity that flashed out of her eyes flattened his face, and she demanded, "Then *say* it," his head jerked backwards, his forehead went up and his eyes stared in fear and she rose and shook her shoulder and arm and fist at him, *"Say* it!"

He stammered, and his body stammered, and he stared at her helplessly, and her face inexplicably shone as metal, and her diamond shaped mouth became the exit for tons of force, and she tilted forward looking up at him, smashed her fist on the bar and screamed "YOU LOVED ME, CAN'T YOU SAY YOU LOVED ME, AND THAT I LOVED YOU YOU SON OF A BITCH?"

And he began to shout at her, he leaned across the bar and

(70)

shook his fist at her, the door opened and the owner of the bar came in, a big man with thin hair and a broad face, eyes brimming with disgust, stepped beside her and took her shoulder and swung her around to face him, put his fist in front of her face and snapped his fingers, *"That's what you're worth,"* he sneered, and he began to curse her, but with hard words, and in a voice tough as oak, and she put both her hands on his chest and shoved him away and he returned and they bitterly cursed each other, the bartender came around from behind the bar and advanced down along the stools and stood beside the entirely distracted man with the mustache and with the owner altogether railed her and she likewise back and it approached crescendo, screaming questions, until in maximum rage she roared did they think she cared now? Why should she care? and she burst into tears, and still they shouted at her, and then she began to shake, her hands and arms and whole body, and face, and lips, shook, and in some kind of verbal inarticulate whirlpool, it blended to snarls and growls, and while they panted and coughed, almost speechless, in the center of her eyes she was hunting lions, and looking at them she said, "At one time, but not now, you scum," and she sat down for a drink, and the owner did too, as the bartender returned to work.

———————————

"Hey honey, like a drink?"

The woman at the jukebox turned, briefly. No. She suppressed a smile; they were old buddies.

The other woman said, louder than before, "What—whaddya mean?" The words went out of the open door with the music, like a silly necklace; she added, strangely, "My husband always said, when you buy somebody a drink, never ask them what they're having."

The woman at the jukebox was smiling and snapping her fingers and moving her feet and hips and the other woman threw her words into the music, "You go hittin' people on the head and then won't take a drink—?" and looked at the man next to her. Her eyebrows arched, her eyes widened, her lips pursed and her shoulders went up; and dropped, her eyebrows smoothed and her eyes folded and a grin split her face. "I love ya," she whispered; and Dinah Washington sang *Funny Thing*.

The younger woman returned to her table passing the older couple saying, mostly to the woman, "I only touched your head."

"Yeah," the woman sneered, and grinned, and looked at her affectionately.

The younger woman grinned back, suppressing a laugh: "A real greeting," she said, and she put her face close up to the other woman's, a little giggly, and wiggled her fingers in the woman's face and breathed, "Hi!"

They wiggled fingers in each other's faces and said Hi! Hi! Hi!

Then the younger woman went to the table where four men sat. She slid in and sat back to the wall looking out between their four heads. Her eyes were tired but she smiled talking to them, her mouth was small and her nose was long and thin, her face was flat, and her red hair, severely banged, gave her face a long triangular look, in pink, with a pointed chin. Dinah Washington's song rose toward its conclusion and the woman stood up on the seat of the booth, and as the men helped her up and laughed self-consciously she looked up towards the ceiling, eyes on an upward angle and out beyond herself, she began to hum and shimmy, and speaking over their heads, beyond even them, yet speaking down to them, too, she was laughing and grinning, warmly gazing upwards, lips moving to the words, funny, funny thing.

(72)

FREEZING PEOPLE

"Bright are the stars that shine
Dark is the sky
I know this love of mine
Will never die
And I love her."

—The Beatles

THE CRYSTAL SOUL of the great poet arched toward her and he buried his head in his hands weeping. Unable to be hers.

She stood a slender five feet eight; her face was pockmarked and her eyes held a glitter which responded to the friction of inner selves; she spread her legs and a different man slid in, etc., and the great poet wept at his separated worlds; his children cavorted around him and his wife washed the dishes.

His soul winged to his pockmarked woman who would not have him; he spread the wings of his city toward her.

He had taken her hand; they had sat at the table in the bar, and holding her fingers spoke to her, upwards she flew away, looking down at him.

"I can't be mother to your children," she said killing him. "I'm incompetent."

A cascade of tears ran down behind his face; "I love you," he said.

"I know," she truly said, "and I know I am not a mother," casting a shadow.

Yet his soul flew to that gloomy dampness—he would move his writer's soul and bloody male heart to the cruelty of her darkness beyond her challenge. He dreamed of her, she walked in him; she walked in him and he leaned to her as the boy-

Beatles sang—he went to her on wings, killing him.

Children raced down the streets as Beatles sang, and girls screamed in circles.

We are all there, no—I am, not you, like her, like me, and her in me, or like me—no, like her in me in "him" behind "his" face, and his or my life, and—his life—that *I am in love with him* via the creamy skinned blonde—pockmarked to be *sure*— I see in the mirror as I shave: looking hard out of my eyes for a perfect icy love.

MOBIUS STRIP

THE NEGRO IN SLACKS and white shirt stood at the bar near the door, beside Sheila (she was wearing her madras shift); a white guy stood on the other side of Sheila drinking whiskey and soda. It was a sweltering smoky night in Greenwich Village and everybody was drunk, and he came on, and though he didn't know if she liked it, she liked it: wasn't he paying attention to her and wasn't he forceful? So she stood a little closer beside him at the bar, and he said, affectionately,

"You know what I dig the most about you baby is how much I hate you."

They looked at each other across her, and then in a heating time-consciousness he laughed, was there going to be an incident? The girl clung to him whispering don't don't

"Don't what, baby?"

But his eyes were on the other, and pupils contracted to a top of laughter and emotion—you take her and I'll be jealous! I'll take her and hate you, and hate her, and hate me!

I'll be jealous—still!

He woke with a Godly erection, against her, and startling her as she woke, momentarily, and then biting his shoulder, and clinging to his buttocks to, give him, bring him into her with her hands, greater drive, in, and their hips swung side to side perspiring in the sultry smoke, minds blank, deleted, in perfect dual orgasm, were one.

"There is nothing," she said, the next day at work, "like making it with a Spade." Spade was the Village word, and her pal Kate was wide eyed.

"You mean—?"

"Sure," Janet said. "I mean, I met him at a bar, and why not; you white people will never see the light. You're too jealous."

"But—" Katie gasped, "—you're white, too!" and then crimsoned in anger and embarrassment: "So am I!"

"Sure," said Janet, lower lip out: "Sure, but with that—I'd rather be with him. I don't think about race, with him. I'm all his."

That night in their apartment the two girls talked, and after watching TV, fell asleep. The next day he phoned her; Katie was out with a friend and so he came over and though Janet wanted him again, he said he didn't feel like it wasn't it too hot? Later. No, then, okay. So they went for a walk in Washington Square where his friends were, and he introduced her, two Negroes and a white guy, and they all talked alike and she figured her pussy was how they were, he had been too. He was getting two ice cream sticks, and she sat with his friends, as her mind opened. Really! White people were—crazy! These people—Spades were the only people in the world, why cry around about it? Let's get together, and she felt warm.

The white guy left them, coolly; she didn't like him.

She was faint in the hands of Negroes, and she sat, flanked by the sexual men—as Baldwin had said! Far more powerful than white men—and white men feared them! And were jealous! No wonder. "How right he is!" she thought, "How knowing! A great sexual writer!"

But she had thought the word they—*them,* and in alarm asked herself—what does it mean? But—there was—Katie! Coming across the Square towards her.

Katie shyly said, "Hi."

Janet smiled in the company of the powerful men, and Katie

said she had to hurry, Janet let her go.

But then later, of course it happened, and they were all friends in Greenwich Village, and things were on the upswing and people staggered around town in the heat, a white guy sat on a stool and ordered some scrambled eggs; he was a little drunk, but in a happy mood; a Negro girl took the order, and when his eggs were given him he grinned to her, and she smiled, and he ordered coffee, she suggested black, yes, he agreed, black would be best, yet as the coffee was scalding hot, he asked for cream, touched on the arm by a very fat white man who called the waitress honey, and as he felt his heart and mind go heavy the waitress responded likewise and without hesitation and gave the fat man his order, giving a pitcher of cream to the other guy; their eyes met, and for a moment, seriously held.

There was no question of contact, but she gave him, a split second look of fierce hostility, and as he had pushed the tip across to her, he reacted visibly: his face went flat in surprise, his eyes were wide, she wheeled the other way, and he finished his coffee, stuttered goodnight, and left, confused and hurt, so then angry—that he had given her the big tip; well, he later sighed, who knows what's going on, foolishly misunderstanding her resentment; why get so serious. Leave me alone.

All white people were guilty, and afraid, so he rejected her, and headed down toward Sheridan Square angrily yet sorry— lonely; they weren't the same, and under his skin his red blood flowed hot, he went in the bar and ordered a beer, and drank it, moodily by the door. A white chick entered, and as the space to his right was free, she stood there, and ordered a whiskey sour. He rejected her in his continuity, precisely as he turned toward her, and waited until she turned, she did, he looked into her eyes and smiled, bitterly, a lovely trip in red with a white

(77)

girl; man, in a slow upward spiral his hate swirled.

He kept coming on there beside her, to her, slender in a madras shift, soft breasts, excitable eyes beside that white cat—

"You know what I dig the most about you baby."

The white guy turned, and looked at him; their eyes met, and held, as she stammered,

"I—I don't know what you mean—"

The white guy said, to her,

"He means he hates you."

"Don't what, baby?"

Eye to eye.

SPACE GATE

THEY RACED DOWN the pitch black corridor toward the distant space gate.

In an ultra-violet light, the walls were lined with eyes: petulant, accusing, and enraged, dilated and pinpointed with unspoken feelings against me, and I was terrified, yet the tall figure of the detective slanting at my side rapidly moving with me, was strong and dramatic and he knew, he need not fear. The two of them ran down the corridor of the eyes, towards the space gate.

Something whiplike was chasing the boy and he cried out, and the detective was on his own then, racing onward—to get there! Get there—fast! FAST!

Alone! A viperous thing at his heels—he called for him! And woke in darkness, the eyes yet burning at him, jumped out of bed, and with the eyes glowing and expanding and contracting and fading he ran down the hallway, through the living room, up the stairs and got in bed beside her, snuggling up.

"Mother!"

Her sleeping world stirred and woke to embrace him, whispering soft as scent,

"Did you have a nightmare?"

"Yes," he wept, and stammered that it had been terrible; she drew him to her and he put his head on her breast and wept as she caressed him; he put his arms around her waist in Paradise.

The eyes, however, did not stop burning, and the thing at his heels yet pursued him, and he snuggled so close to his mother in terror and need it was as if he would enter her and flow along with her, and he shuddered because the thing that chased him was growing unnaturally large.

And close. Moving the hair on his body, it had the color of human brains and the texture of fog, it was as large as summer rain, mossy and deep with death. The boy gasped on his mother's breast, as she murmured to him. Her breasts and neck and stomach were warm from the power of her sleep, and her skin was the surface above her steady and circulating richness of red where he longed to hide he shook as the dead brain fog breathed on him, he opened his eyes.

Across the landscape of rising and falling breasts under her nightgown, and just beyond the open door to her room, in the recess of the gloomy hallway above the stairs, a solitary outraged eye floated, its look scissored through his eyes and cut at his mind as he threw his head from side to side,

"STOP! STOP!" eyes shut.

"What is it—?"

"I DON'T KNOW—AN EYE! STOP LOOKING! STOP WATCHING ME!"

He was in a shuddering fit and she held him as he shook, and she murmured—

"THE EYE!" he screamed, "AND THE GRAY IS NEAR!"

She whispered, "I am here."

His muscles went slack as he sighed, and in a moment he was asleep.

She shut off the light, he woke, he evoked the deadness and the furious eye jiggled, he seized her.

"THE LIGHT! TURN ON THE LIGHT!"

She did. He was Evoking it.

"We must sleep, sweetheart."

He was stunned by his power of Evocation.

Mother fell asleep; animal boy perspired on her nightgown. Her arm was around him, his arms were around her neck. He put his face into the swirling draw of deep soft pillows.

—Where was the detective!

He looked over his shoulder to where the light was dim. He looked across his sleeping mother at the floating eye in the hallway and a chill swept through him, he averted his eyes. He lowered his head and closed his eyes.

He gave his heart, and the eye took dimensional regression—and they were together.

They raced down the corridor of eyes, towards the space gate—they ran! RUN—to get there! Get there! Fast—FAST!

The tall figure of the detective slanting at my side, unfearing, far far ahead: the doorway, night and the space gate, with all the stars beyond.

THE NEWS

GOD I HATE WOMEN! Oh the dumb MYSTERY of unconscious cunning smiles, dogs with split snakes in their souls. "I want to hear the news," my mother writes, hungry again.

I sneer at beautiful somnambulists, numbskull bitches floating—probably laterally—and the way I see it, on a slow decline—through their lives . . . playing out their endless stereotyped roles, God it is so dull and unimportant, my GOD I'M SICK of their needs, and their looking-glass chaos appearing in a million daily clichés, while men—the clowns of existence, real jokers, crawl behind, tongues hanging out for just a little of *that*.

Yes baby, you've got your liberty, your freedom in this vague society is firmly established. You can do anything you want. Go to a movie by yourself, or with a girlfriend, or with some trapped guy, and afterwards, just as before, you can go home, or go to a bar, you can fuck or not fuck and sooner or later you'll fall asleep, well, you have to do that, and somewhere along the line, pretty invisible, you will what you call wake up, and begin the next day as you began the one before, time is difficult to chart, but anyway, what the hell; I can see your face now; you don't like that—remember your expression? Of course not. Your face like shattered glass. You were. Also helpless. Well I saw you a couple of weeks later, and in the dim light and dark crowd around that screaming jukebox, your frightened words, "I died last night," brought today and tomorrow into electric clearness, and when I told you you *must* take care, you nodded, mute; you lowered your eyes and a moment later threw yourself into the arms of a dozen sleepwalking men, making all the other guys across this stinking nation really *green* with envy.

RED IMPACT

I WAS DRINKING BEER in a bar on lower 3rd Avenue and idly staring at that Miller High Life anxiety gadget, as its brightly colored lines wove and looped and twisted in an endless-seeming pattern.

The bartender, Jimmy, a patient goon type, was wiping the bar and in a sense I had the eye on him which he knew, and he seemed carelessly pleased, we had a relationship of sorts, a waiting one; after I'd had a dozen or two he generally gave me one on the house.

It was a dull night. I was sitting near the door, and as the bar was small, when the door opened and the man and the girl came in and stood at the end of the bar, they were almost at my side, and the handful of people at the bar looked.

He was about five ten, and slender with a flat face and careful little ice gray eyes, and I hated and feared him immediately. He was dressed in a gray double breasted suit, pressed neat, a white shirt and pale gray and red diagonally striped tie, and as he looked along the bar at Jimmy, I saw his nails were manicured. He was at least forty-five.

The girl was as tall as he was, but young, not over twenty, and the American prototype: long light brown hair, beautifully modeled face on a skull that rose in back, like an Irish Setter's skull, she was slender, poised, and beautifully dressed, yet there was something dog-like in her expression as she stood beside him; with her eyes down like that, she was having an effect on the bar.

Jimmy ambled down and stood in front of the man, and pleasantly smiled, Yeah? as the man looked Jimmy directly in the eyes without hardly moving his lips, the man put his right index finger on the bar square in front of the girl, and then moving his finger and putting it on the bar in front of himself, he said,

"Two Johnny Walker Red on the rocks."

He had an accent.

Jimmy made the drinks, and set them on the bar as directed and the man paid him, Jimmy rang it up and began wiping shotglasses and watching as the man turned to the girl, he turned completely, and facing her, with his glass in his hand, but very casually, he said,

"Drink."

She took a sip of her drink. So did he.

I lit a cigarette in a muted alarm, put my head in my left hand, stared at the bar, took a drink of my beer, like he had told me to, and cleared my throat and glanced at Jimmy. Jimmy had moved to the far end of the bar and stood in a shadow, watching. He glanced at me. I glanced at the girl and the man in the gray suit; at his flat face. He was a foreigner, and his gray eyes swung from her face and gazed directly at me with a touch of amusement, though his lips were tight, but he was completely at ease.

She, however, stood as a fine creature with lowered eyes, her lovely hand around her drink on the bar, standing beside her master. Her shoulders were slumped a little forward. Her hair had fallen a little, following the forward tilt of her head so it framed her face in a very fashionably sad way and I couldn't bear it any longer. I got up and offered her my barstool. She didn't move. The foreigner said, softly to her,

"Where are your manners? If as this gentleman has, someone offers you a seat, you accept, and you sit. *Sit down.*"

Most subtly she shook her head. No. He made a faint

smile. And firmly:

"*Sit.*"

She sat down.

Then the foreign man looked at me. His gray eyes became hammered and angular, oblique, and my heart froze as his smile spread, and then I went rigid—as his words,

"You are very kind," vanished in the collective gasp from the others at the bar, as his dense gray mica eyes sparkled above a spreading stainless steel-toothed grin.

THERE IS A MAN I KNOW

THERE IS A MAN I know. His eyes are green, his hair is brown and streaked with gray. He has a youthful look because his nose is turned up, he will be thirty-seven this August, his favorite color is blue, his skin is white, he is six feet tall, weighs 175 pounds, likes denim pants and cotton shirts, he walks fast in long strides, he's a summer man, and a popular person at the bar; the back of his head is rather flat, and his face projects forward blade-like.

Except for the times now when he is lost, in his anger and unhappiness, he is always going somewhere, and he loves women, but these days he drinks too much Russian vodka—which he loves—and in the awesome power of human earthquake—heartbreak—he is impotent these days, and there is a peculiar quality of self pity and heroism he identifies with, never knowing which he is, and he is both, and in a sense he is also slightly spellbound. And hurt.

A few weeks ago he was making love with Large Flower. She is a kind woman, but in a deep thrust he realized the sound of a cliché—he was killing the time he needed to extricate himself from his ex-wife, *kill* frightened him, he lost his erection, and until last night he was impotent, every woman reminding him of the word time he needed to *kill* to extricate himself, etc., and he went in a child rage/confusion and blurred idea of heaping time into kill into wife into women, and one afternoon when he was drunk he bought a papier-mâché Mexican Death Mask in a Baseball Cap, and then he went into the

Village and bought a God's Eye, handwoven violet and blue cotton yarn, and he put the Mexican Death Mask in a Baseball Cap on the wall over his pillow, and a few inches to the left he hung the Eye of God, and in a peculiar way generally indicating rebirth, he let the Mexican Death Mask in a Baseball Cap, a big toothy painted wild-eyed grin—affect him, and he let the Eye of God handle it, and with the odd regressive trust of the talisman, he began to understand that he could handle the violence of his emotions which so often these days have brought him to death, and last night, I gave him—I gave this man I know the grace of his identity. And this morning I placed him in his time.

He had cried out looking in. I gave him two primary words last night, and this morning I gave him myself: I alone, in his name the slightly alchemical woman: will save him.

1:

I've realized so many things these last few days, it's a little hard to live in any kind of peacefulness, but at least, in a fragment of peace now, let me thank you—really, with all my heart. If you hadn't given me the words, I —well, I would have left her. I like Large Flower, and it would have disappointed her deeply, had I gone away. I would have—my pride, or what's left of it—comes first, as you know. I would have gone to the bar and let my broken heart get further wrecked by that Goddess Waitress so faithful to her slick and unfaithful husband—she is very unhappy; her hands are warm, and her fingers are slender, the perfect extensions of her slender nearly royal figure; it's all a little hopeless, and I'm probably falling in love again, and I swore I wouldn't, oh does it ever end? I know it doesn't. And when Large Flower bent towards my face, I was in—dig—the director's chair, by the table, the candles were lit, I took her large naked breasts in my hand, I remember the panic I felt, the tumbling regret—the awful a priori—remember how I cried in to you?

Yes.

And you—you came through, I unzipped my fly and *desperately* said: *touch me*. She did, and oh how I came up, alive, awake, returning from all the painful places, I the magic prince; we made terrific love.

Yet then in the night my ex-love stepped into my consciousness in all her remembered gloryness, and such perfect coldness—which had chilled me so many times, chilled/killed, I remember her icy base back, and the words you gave me—my own words—*touch me,* broke the ice, are you the woman I need don't answer that, no, but you *are* the warmth, that other chill must go, I want to come up green, but God it's tough—remember when she bought the red dress and we went to that party and on the way asked me if I liked her new dress and I told her about the lady and John Dillinger, and she laughed, and that night left the party with another guy—pile time into kill into wife, life: death, true good Eye of God, but *Christ* it hurts, *wow* it's tough—

2:

I hardly slept at all last night, but when I came out of the doze, around six thirty a.m. I felt guilty about Large Flower; I felt that—I was using her—baby that type of voice is your evil sister—well, but—maybe I am!

But not wrongly!

Yes! It's—it's just it, I get very shook when she weeps afterwards, where does it come from, and why? Is it—is it that she's I mean I know she's an orphan, but *is* it that, and that in orgasm, her orgasm is deep, she lets go, does she touch an old identity, and then, in sleep which follows soon, she copes and weeps and dozes and wakes having missed the self she touched so briefly, and weeps again?

About 7:15, dawn in New York, I had a cigarette and thought about that, and it somehow all came together and I was angry that I had talked about my mother last night, knowing Large Flower was an orphan, I mean sitting in bed while she was asleep I thought I'd come home and write this.

That felt great, and I began putting it together, and she got up, and made us coffee (mine with a drop of vodka), and while she took a bath I felt it come into my fingertips. I enjoy being in her apartment, it's lovely—small, but individual because she cares. I'm not sure she likes it, wishes it was bigger etc., I can feel a guilt come up about commitment, but she has none to me, so we're straight ahead, and I

said so long at the subway entrance there on
Cooper Square, and she went to work, and I
came home, thinking I was in it—in rhythm—
and after breakfast I lay alone on my bed, and
you slowly in your way, which is sudden to me,
occurred to me, and offered yourself as alter-
nate to the figure of woman as Time or Death,
so—deeply—thank you. In despair, I know I
can turn to you, regardless of that retail import
from Mexico, and with the help of the other retail import from Mexico, it's no secret I need—
you—I mean—you know—yes—

Yes. You're tired. Rest now. Rise, later.

UP IN NEW ENGLAND

THAT NIGHT she was asking the tall man in the blue sweatshirt to make her a whiskey sour, as Grandad sat in the rocker by the window in the kitchen laughing at Grandma's shyness; the younger woman asked the man in the blue sweatshirt,

"Aw come on, please don't be angry, we're all a little drunky. Would you. Would you be?" and she added "from Broadway, huh?"

The man in the blue sweatshirt glanced at his wife who looked at him levelly.

"All right," he said, and made the drink.

That afternoon the woman who later begged him for the drink, had told her son to run upstairs and get her sweater, which he obediently did, and then rejoined his friend and they began to play cards, and his mother began to get drunk, and later she asked à la New York for the man to make her a drink, and he did.

But she was then making Donald Duck noises, and twisting her long hair around her face like a mustache, and just before a late supper when Grandpa was lifting Grandma's pullover and began licking her back while the others laughed, the boy's mother began to shout recklessly, and anxiously, to sit down for supper, turn off that fucking television and sit down for supper, tensely, they did, and after a strange forced meal she told her son and his friend to take a walk outside, the night was beautiful, and they obediently did, and after a few minutes as the adults stood around the stove in the New Hampshire chill, the boys returned, and in the candlelight in the wooden kitchen, he saw their faces, more relaxed, and somewhat cool, as they came in, in their eyes, as her son said he was glad it had stopped raining, the eyes of the man in the blue sweatshirt sharpened—did he see a trace, just a trace, of the other boy's lips glowing on her son's lips?

LEO'S TUNE

I returned to the land
where I was loved,
it was once in a while—a dream—
alone with my changed
face and eyes
and silver hair.
Structures were being built
and I spoke with
to shake hands again—with—
I was a stranger
in their faces and eyes
walls and bridges
my dearest friends
and they had worked on beyond me
in the lonely land of experience
where the I things change
all day through
walking
of—invisible roads
to be gone beyond
as I returned—following

THE OLD MAN

For Mario and Helen

"Just a moment, young man."

The writer turned on edge. A man, at least seventy, was sitting dapper and alone in a shadow at a table, drink before him. The old man said,

"Would you join me for a moment?"

The writer looked at him fearfully. The man's eyes were steady circles, not unfriendly and not warm; they made a camera shutter click at two youths at the bar, who pivoted on their stools to face him. The elderly man flicked his hand.

"You can go now; I'm all right."

The two youths moved toward the writer, black eyes glistening punk-sparkle; and the writer, threatened, yet rose in reaction to his fear of them and his hatred of them, glared at them furiously. They stopped, one on each side of him—and the writer was startled by a disappearance of fear in an air, a dumb air they exuded, of strange opposites: two boys like mute, white, vulnerable, and softly dangling, feminine penises. Irritation riffled the old man's features, and he said,

"Oh stop playing. Go, I'm all right."

They murmured in amusement like sleeping girls, and slipped out.

The dapper man smiled to the writer. "Come. Sit here." He cast a string, caught the writer and he went to him on it; Pinocchio sat down. The man said,

"Would you like a drink?"

The painted writer nodded. The man rose, and at the bar

ordered drinks, but the writer was angrily beside him with fifty cents on the bar.

"I'll get this," the man said.

"No. You pay for yours, I'll pay for mine."

"Won't you let me buy you a drink?"

"Never."

"Have it your way, then."

"I will."

They returned to the table with drinks. The man said, "I heard you talking about Viet Nam."

The situation was familiar, and in his fear and anxiety he remembered one time he had let a man pick him up like this—no, not like this at all, but an old threat to end it—or aimed at him *with* his sex, was still there. They had gone to a black and white chrome Hollywood hotel and had a grimy sexual night. He had stolen money from the man the following morning, and run away. No manner of suppression could keep it under the floor, and it seeped upward through the cracks and made him damp, and smell musty, haunted, and the doctor had asked him who it was, unblinking. The writer had said he had been lonely for contact. Contact with—? The writer had angrily answered, oh I know, sure, but that only makes it—. The doctor had then said,

"Do you want to see it now? Or later?"

The writer had said, quickly, "Okay, it's my father, but I don't want sex with my father, my father is dead, I never knew my father, he was always away."

"But, then, who did you—or do you, want?"

"I want my wife!"

"Why can't you have her? Is it someone else?"

"She won't—"

"Answer me."

"I don't know, but—oh yes, Mother!"

"You fear *him*. Who is he?"

"Probably father, while I suckle mother's breast."

"You're not listening."

"Yes I am."

"Why can't you hear me?"

"I can—oh, I see. Ha hahaha," and the writer remembered when he was a boy he watched his mother comb her long white hair in front of a mirror. Occasionally she had glanced bewitchingly at him in the mirror, and chanted.

> *Rapunzel, Rapunzel*
> *Let down your golden hair*

The doctor had asked, "Didn't you tell me you had become 'the man of the house' after your father died?"

The writer had nodded. "Yes. I proclaimed I was, but when my aunts echoed it with amusement, it was different. I felt I had double-crossed a liberty I had made for myself. Or I felt my aunts did, double-crossed the identity I had made for me, casting away my father *I* was the man, of *this* house with my mother. But then I saw what I had said, or what they thought I meant, which was responsibility: I had proclaimed I would accept all the manly responsibilities of the house, and it finished me. I had sealed myself in, but they used it on me for years."

"In."

"In a twelve year old game of playing Man/Me."

"They saw your role from their eyes—"

"Yes, that would be your word; they saw their boy nephew playing the role of the man of the house."

"All right, but weren't you the man even before your father died? While he was away you were in your mother's room watching her comb her hair, and she sang to you. Can you see your father from that angle? What would happen if he came home and found you there?"

"It would—"

"It?"

"Okay, *he* would wreck—what—I had going."

"Do you know what it was? And who is the man in the street you fear? Or the man you had the homosexual relations with?"

He began to fall backwards in a warm feminine wave suckling whiteness and water and cream scent, softness and security filled him, crying out,

"The light is bright!"

"Easier to sleep with a man than to fight him, as you say: fear blocks experience, so every act to make to be a man is threatened by the lurking *one*, who will appear to destroy the man you're afraid to be. Coming from a mother's warmth to father's fury you fear so greatly you return to her, a little like a woman, even with a man, rather than face the man with the man you are, and you are *very* angry."

Unted States Policy in Southeast Asia, walking down University Place. The writer asked,

"Have you ever read Jung?"

"Freud's early friend?"

"Yes. Jung says the shadow is the same sex as its owner."

"What are you telling me? I wasn't talking about that!"

Pinocchio said, "I am."

"What do you do for a living!"

"I have a job with an importing firm."

"Is it a good job?"

"Yes," woodenly.

"What else do you do—are you an artist, a poet?"

He had no life, no sex, no mind and the street went on forever. He said,

"I am, a fiction writer."

The man smiled. "Fiction! Good."

An angry tape unwound. "Fiction: truth the way it isn't lived."

"Ha ha, that's good. You know, I like you."

He stopped in his tracks. His knees knocked together and his wooden jaws clattered, his painted eyes were wide as he pointed up the street:

"You go ahead. I'm going home."

"Don't be ridiculous, come for a cup of coffee."

Stainless steel, formica and lettered signs: the counterman in Rikers gave them coffee. The writer was dizzy, nauseous and exhausted, he yawned and drank some of the hotness, it was good. Something came clear. He turned to the man.

"I want to tell you something."

The dapper man looked at him with his cool but not unfriendly eyes. He could manipulate men and stay clean to himself, which explained the slight mocking smile: I want to tell you something was nothing new.

"You bring my past to me."

"How so?" Surprised.

"You resemble a dark fellow I fear."

"What are you trying to say!"

The writer was a little startled, and as he began, the man interrupted him with an angry hiss:

"My God! Don't tell me you're another young *faggot!* I'm *sick* of them!" He paused. "Is that it?" Angrily.

They looked in each other's eyes and laughed, seeing their selves on strings, and a subtle watery glitter covering each's eyes, and the writer reacted first, despising his own water, which the dapper man seemed to enjoy in himself.

The writer said, tight-lipped, "Now I don't like you completely."

(98)

"But—why? Why?"

"You look like a crook I know—"

"Come, come," the man angrily interrupted, "really, now; don't be naive, you don't know anything about me."

"Yeah," the writer sneered, "not about you, but—I'm going home. You scare me, I'm tired of complicity and ill with me."

"But why are you afraid of me?"

"You remind me of me, which is a threat."

"I'm not going to hurt you."

"Not like the others, or me, anyway. And how do you know?"

"What are you saying?"

"I'm going home. Goodnight."

"Finish your coffee. Sit down."

"No. I'm exhausted."

"Sit down, come on. Finish your coffee, then I'll go my way and you go yours."

Pinocchio sat down gloomily, defensive and emotional. The dapper man said,

"You're an extraordinary young man."

"For Christ's sake! I'm fucked up! And thirty-five is *not* young!" He turned vehemently on the man, "You're twice my age and we understand each other exactly, how about *that!*"

The man laughed for a moment; "From where I sit, that is not a mundane statement."

They were both surprised, and both grinned.

"See? You can be pleasant."

"You really grab at straws, don't you?"

"I wanted to talk with you. . ."

"No, with someone."

"All right; true, but I listened to what you were saying about Viet Nam, and it so happens—" but the writer's face had darkened, and the man paused, asking what was wrong.

"Please, don't go through it again."

"What! I also read what Carey McWilliams wrote this week! Ha, ha, the old goat is not *all* stupid!"

"Goats terrify me."

"Ah—this is ridiculous."

It was as if the writer stood up in himself, he stood up and stepped away from the counter stool and looked levelly angry down at the dapper man, who shuddered. The writer gravely said:

"You condescend and make me helpless so you can manipulate me. I don't like that. I know you because I know myself. I don't know, however, why I'm here. I was drawn here. Why am I here? I'm hysterical! Shall I throw the coffee cup through the window there? Or shall I strike myself? How shall I show my anger? Shall I hit *you?* Don't you see what you do? No. Do you see what you are? No. You're a manipulator, and the stereotype upper echelon crooked politician with a shadowy past."

The dapper man lowered his eyes, and stared at the floor; he said softly, emotionally, "I'm sorry you said that."

The writer gasped, and stammered, "Me too, now! Me too, and what does *that* mean? That's a THREAT to me, you can't talk like that to paranoids, we'll run out of here screaming! You don't want to be hurt? Me neither, so you blind well-dressed fool, can't you see it's my role to hurt you to get at me, can't you see that? I don't know *you* in you, but in me, I know —I've boozed in too many Village bars for too many years not to know you when you show up. When you're like you, you have to show up, so every now and again you come in the door to have a talk with writers or artists, and you mean well, you're a little bored with your jungle life and want some honest neurotic people that understand that you're lonely while you buy us drinks, but you will somehow threaten them because just the way you are you bring them a story they know and fear, you can't walk into a world where guys are crazy *because* they're artists, you want the real thing, you want to meet the guy who can't help but paint, and you can spot a phoney—snap?—but they—we—fear your hunger for the real because we are so real that way ourselves, it's our *norm*. How do you expect us to pass truth on to you when it's all we can do to admit it to ourselves and then live with it. Your act is a venomously vicarious one, and deeply hypocritical, which will be met with resentment, awe, fear and anger in the men you most want to talk with, not because you are *you*, as you fool yourself into thinking, but because your mind and emotions are starved, but your habit is manipulation, and you are, in your way, tragically screwed, and when you appear before us, we see it, what we know by heart, miserably familiar."

The writer tossed fifteen cents on the counter and left, hearing the dapper man say,

"I'll never forget that."

And he hated that response because he couldn't yet accept what he had just said, if he knew, and he stormed along the streets striking fist against palm, and had he been another substance, say sulfur, he would have smoked, from rage and fear, and when he got home he threw his clothes off his body and collapsed into bed as the two punks beat him in an alley because the dapper old man had said he would be sorry, he fought helplessly, and bitterly, in loneliness and a deep grief sensing a figure across his dark loft, gazing at the writer's wrenching body, a man with a white and yellow sunny face and wings who gestured in care, regret, and sorrow for the figure of unhappiness on the bed, speaking,

"Sorry for you,"

dripping sweat the writer wept in confusion and futility—

he called out for help, a tearful mutter, and the angel came close, the writer was aware of grace and slowly slipped through smoke into darkness, wiping his eyes he let his head sink into the damp pillow, sleep, the angel said, kindly aware of his wife's warm sleeping body next to his sleep, the gentle voice said, finally,

"Sleep."

THE MAN IN THE GROUND

HE SPOTTED THE POET LATELY, at the bar, and they embraced each other warmly, laughing hello in smoke and shadows and had a drink.

The writer drank compulsively because he feared the dreams he had written—he hated his cowardice: he melted into the icy booze.

But the poet Lately was guzzling double bourbons as a self-conscious comic machine and the poet Lately was not.

Cool, bright, deductive; in the past the writer, feeling lonely, had sought him out to talk with him, and though the poet always seemed to understand, in a way of being pleased, was visibly patient, and the writer felt a guilt using his friend so, and yet kept on talking, the poet's eyes were becoming resentful, and it came about in the conversation that the poet knew Carraday, an old friend, and the writer wondered why he hadn't known that the poet and Carraday were friends, and he felt dizzy as the poet, in a pointed way, became interested in the writer's relationship with Carraday, schoolmates the writer smiled, was the poet Lately jealous? No. He didn't smile, he fell darkly silent, he—the poet—turned to the bar and gazed through smoke into his drink.

The writer began to realize he didn't know the poet at all, he had only used him and his ear. The writer was embarrased and regretful, and turned, introspectively, to leave, but the poet, looking at him, spoke his name normal and friendly.

"So what's new?"

It was the one the writer knew. Anxious to get things going

again, the writer said several things were happening, and he began to tell them, yet every thing he said was personal, and though the poet understood because it was the writer talking, the poet could not understand fully because each thing was personal, and the poet, as the writer talked, pointed things out, things the writer had mentioned in the years before, though the writer did not intend it that way, the writer said yes, in anxiety, and when the writer, not knowing what to say that was new and would bring them together mentioned a mutual friend the poet's face once again darkened, and he became hostile, as the writer realized the poet has heard that before, yet the writer became irritated because the poet was or seemed to be listening in revenge with a different motive.

"Why doesn't he tell you to shut up?"

"Do you think a relationship is someone listening to you?"

The poet had again turned gloomily away. The writer nervously said,

"I said I saw Carraday. I'm not going into the whole thing again because I—know, I mean I know—" and the first person stung, the writer carrying out his sentences: "I know you've already heard it."

"But this is something different, if I can talk it, and I'd like you to—"

The poet glared at him and turned away disgusted. The writer dropped his eyes muttering okay, and ordered another drink, the poet turned to him.

"What happened?"

"He didn't recognize me."

"Who didn't."

The writer looked at the poet. "Don't you know?"

The poet made a tight smile. "I know."

"He didn't recognize you."

"He saw me, he looked right in my eyes and didn't recognize me—he was preoccupied of course. Yet it was—*it was from another time—*"

The poet gave the writer a hard directly hostile look. He said, "I know about you and his wife," and the poet made his deduction.

The writer was taken aback, and angry, and for a moment looked at the poet in silence.

"I must have told you when I was drunk, or maybe he told you, it was years ago. There was none of that in his eyes when I saw him last week. It was as if—"

"I know about you and his wife," the poet repeated bitterly.

"You son of a bitch telling me again and not letting me finish my sentence."

The poet said through a smile, "Am I right? Or am I wrong?"

"Wrong," and he saw the poet flush in rage; "wrong in unexplained motives, and wrong in—" but the poet interrupted him and the writer interrupted, "Look, hey, what's happening? Something's—tell me, will you?" The poet had interrupted, however, with a cherub's smile and fiery eyes. "You're angry, you want to hurt me."

The writer cried, "I want to get things straight! Tell me! Tell me!"

"Too late," the poet smiled gently. "You want to hurt me," and he touched his lower lip: "Hit me."

"Hit me, there." He gave the writer a shrewd look. "Remember, I don't fall down."

The writer grabbed the poet's shoulders and shook him. "You're out of your head," he angrily said. "D'ya hear me?"

The poet grinned behind tight lips: "I don't fall down."

The writer stepped back, and looked at him. "I do."

The poet mused, "That's the difference between you and

me. That's the real thing."

The writer shook his head, "Wrong again. It's the distance, not difference, between us."

The poet was smiling a coloring mask of violence; the writer frowned, fearing it, and slowly turning, the mask disappeared from him.

A chill rushed through the writer. He began to crumble before a shadow of fear flowing through him, and he scorned himself growing smaller fearing the tall poet. The bar rose slightly and the writer stumbled down to the other end of it and leaned on it dizzily, and he was very angry, and identities in emotion charged up; he wanted to vomit.

He did not in a flash of rage, and—something peculiar, a breeze, wafted near his temples. I'm drunk out of my wits, he mumbled; "Tomorrow then, I'll tell you, for it is coming." The writer hardly heard, yet behind himself,

"Not what. Who."

The writer finished his drink quickly with a twisted face, terrible shit, whiskey, he grunted, stomach convulsing, anxious, in a dream

all the Men are coming to get me

He flushed crimson, his heart banged boiling blood throughout as perspiration started down his forehead, he ordered another drink, lit a cigarette trembling and rapidly swallowing suppressed nausea, huddled in his clothing against the wind.

All the Men

He knew, and the cold wind swirled around his temples, chilling the perspiration, he froze on his feet. His red brow turned white in a new alarm and his new blood ran cold, the glass clattered against his teeth and he turned, to face the poet Lately directly. The poet had an ugly mask in his hand; the writer said, but the poet interrupted him.

"Where have you been."

"Here," the writer said, the voice said. With one hand he gestured the poet away, "You won't listen. I refuse you."

The writer walked away, to a wall and leaned against it, while the poet sat at the bar and peered dismally into his drink. He turned, and looked sadly at the writer who was talking with a reporter. The poet said he would listen. He did, for a while. but again slanted into the other, and the writer again walked away.

David Henderson was sitting in back and they greeted each other warmly. It had been a long time. David looked weary and poor in worn denim. He gazed, as exhausted, at the (fiction) writer, who said, "You look terrible. Want a drink?"

"I have some money," the young poet said.

The writer stood up and waved at the waiter, and sitting down, asked, "What have you been doing? Workin' on de railroad?"

The writer cackled and the young poet smiled, and said he had been writing a lot, and was starting on a circuit of readings which would take him over the country including the south. The writer said, "The south?"

The young poet said bitterly, "This city's cold, baby, weatherwise; otherwise freezing."

"The south?"

"The sun," David smiled, "is warm in the south."

The waiter appeared and they ordered drinks and talked until the bar closed.

And as the writer wove towards the door the poet Lately grabbed him, and they staggered home parting on a blue side-street. The poet Lately threw an empty bottle up Broadway, and it made a smashing echo.

The next day the writer's wife asked him why he hadn't hit

the poet Lately, she said she would have.

"Tough you," the writer said.

"Were you afraid?"

"Yes," he said, ashamed.

Shadow in! And he began to crumble, again—the walls seemed to rise, and he felt himself a little shorter.

"I fear!" he had cried. "But *I* am NOT afraid! Although I CAN be!"

The doctor nodded. "What do you do, when you are."

I run away.

"I run away," he echoed.

"What happened?"

After he finished talking, the doctor asked, "Do you know who it is?"

The writer shrank. The man's eyes were headlamps:

"Who is it you want to hit that you fear and can't hit?"

The writer's back arched, and with his head back, saw eyes closed in a box of a hate of a guilt for a force to kill the father who died, and be rid of them all and write in a rage of the past.

THE FACE IN THE CASKET

In Memory of Paul Blackburn

THEY SAT ON THE MEXICAN RUG beside the colorful pile of presents under the Christmas tree. The writer's wife in her nightgown and housecoat, and himself in pajamas and robe. He poured coffee and suggested she open the first present. She slowly took a large oblong package, undid the ribbon and carefully took off the tissue, and opened the box full of brightly colored rolls of wool, plus two long ivory needles.

Later, he said, "Well, don't you think we should talk about it?"

She murmured she supposed it would be better.

"We could go on the rest of our lives without—" he began.

"—the intrusion," she finished looking at him. Her brown eyes were shadowed. He added: "of talking with him about it."

She nodded and angrily mentioned he had finished what she had already finished. He said he only wanted to finish his sentence. He said if he talked with him it *would* be an intrusion, and he would be the hypocrite, intruding. She agreed.

He asked, "Then why not just let it—go by?"

She asked, "You want to talk to him, don't you?"

He nodded. "I want to intrude and prove a point I don't know."

She said she would rather not, now, talk about it. Would he play something?

A present from the poet Lately, and Ellington and Coltrane softly swirled and swept through the loft, blending with the paintings, drawing, poems and photographs on the walls, and the lovely bright Christmas tree, and all the open presents into the hardship of the writer and his wife in conflict.

"We ought to talk, regardless."

"Regardless of how I feel," she said bitterly.

"In spite of it."

She breathed hard, but she knew he was right. She said she wasn't very delighted to be with him. She would rather be alone. Her-self: alone, she knew he understood, but he hated to see the shadow cast between them, and in her division she was angry at her and self; had she told him the dream? In spite of self and her she envied him in a sharp arrow.

He said energetically, "All right, I'm afraid to say what I think! But I want, I want to say it in the way I'm screwed up in it, and I fear it in the saying—remember in New Hampshire when I couldn't say George's dog was the vehicle for George's suppressed hatred and violence? Granny had to say it for me! Tender, shy, self-conscious George—with a police dog at his heels? Are you ready? How could I say that about George—I know George—old George, I've known and loved George, yet when that dog went after that girl on the street, and I saw George's face—

"Somewhere deep I hate Marko, yes, just like that, and I know I'm crazy but I swear he killed her, I remember her voice on the telephone that day—"

The writer's wife was gravely shaking her head, but the writer raised his trembling hand, "Yes! Sure it's crazy—you just can't *say* things like that about people, but SOMEWHERE I'm RIGHT! I *know* I'm right! Can't you see? I want to tell him I know, I want to intrude into his new life with his new wife and tell him I know something I don't."

"I'm not there at all," the writer's wife said; "you are. Maybe you're right in yourself, at least you feel it, a truth—fact, maybe, and I know you want to be friends again, but I don't; it'd complicate my already complicated life." Her face began to go slack.

He quickly said, stressing last and night, "Why did you dream of him last night!"

She said:

"After the days when I used to hang around with the street gangs, I started to come down from the Bronx to the Village, and I met some people from the Bronx there, who, it turned out, though I didn't know them in the Bronx, lived on the same street I did—you know all this—well, but it was, they were, different from any of the people I'd ever known. They were serious. They were bright—very bright, high IQs etc., and there was a guy who was a painter, he did that—"

He nodded. She pointed to the wall; he knew she meant the little painting of the sea, he didn't look, she smiled, and he said it was the first time she had spoken of these people as a group, he had come to know them through her as specific individuals, not as a group in time.

"The painter was in the army at that time," she continued, "I think. But the others, highschool dropouts, and the rest, guys and girls, were very bright, and we hated the political system, and some of us were pro-Communist. Ann was always there. It was where I met Nathan, and even though I went with him I could never talk with him. The only one I enjoyed talking with was—"

"Marko."

"Yes," she murmured. "Marko was serious in the way I was."

"Way you are."

She nodded. "We understood each other. There was a way I could talk with him and be aware I was talking to him, him

I was aware of, and he was of me to me. It was a way we were—" she gestured—

"Together."

She smiled sadly. "Yes. We had great times. Drinking coffee and talking until late. Then Ann and I'd take the train home. One night we all linked arms and made a Broadway show line in the street—can you imagine it? Outside the Waldorf cafeteria on Sixth Avenue—NEW YORK NEW YORK! we sang." She had her hands out and her face was happy.

She finished her coffee.

"If that why you dreamed about him last night?"

She shrugged.

The writer remembered the night before last: the 23rd. She and her friend Judy had gone out Christmas shopping and had stopped by the bar to see if friends were there, but only saw the old standbys, plus some strangers, and among them the writer's wife had encountered the cartoonist Kingsley, and they had sat at a table and had had a long talk. She had come home at two thirty a.m., beaming, and told the writer about it. He and Kingsley hadn't hit it off at all, and he found himself jealous that Kingsley was attracted to his wife, yet the writer knew jealousy, his jealousy was something he had always felt, a chaotic little whirlpool that grew bigger and drew him in. It frightened him, and then it took his legs away and terrified him pulling him down, yet he seemed to arise in a strength.

The writer leaned forward. "Do you think you dreamed of Marko last night because of your rewarding talk with Kingsley the night before?"

"Mm." She brightened. The writer said,

"Speaking seriously for a prolonged time awakened your relationship with Marko—awakened Marko to you."

"Yes," she said. "That's good. But I—manipulated Kingsley

—so I could speak with him, and when I got him where he could respond, he did, but it still wasn't spontaneous. Kingsley's fucked up."

To vindicate his fluid jealousy, the writer asked,

"Can you speak to me seriously?"

"Sometimes." You jealous baby.

To step out of a dizzy spell, he was redundant, "So you were making it with Nathan, but loving Marko."

It didn't work, and he was angry at himself; she nodded unhappily: "I loved him," she said. The writer was sitting beside himself whispering in his ear, "WRONG! WRONG!" He was coldly watching him looking into his wife's eyes, saying,

"The months after Sherry's funeral had no meaning to me, I felt so dulled, but when we went to Marko's new apartment that night, there was Marko with a new girl, and he was clearly happy, but nothing had changed between you two. I was very drunk, at my worst, but now, no wonder, and there's nothing else to do but say I didn't have any relationship with Marko—ever, and I thought I did. We liked each other very much, possibly loved each other; at times I felt very close to him. I was certain he understood me, although I didn't understand him, I saw him—I was sure he'd make a fine therapist—which you know, and I used to have fantasies of going to him. Wow."

She nodded. She had been aware of that.

"Things yet disturbed me" the writer went on, "and the day when Marko and Sherry and their kids met us in the park, and we were all together, there were a few things happening.

"You and Marko were together and I was with Sherry. But —remember just after we were married? I felt a little strange about visiting them, there was something contradictory I was never conscious of. I would see Marko, and Sherry, and the

(113)

kids, but—I mean, I—was the one outside—something, the plot, look inside your head a little and listen and remember. It was like going into a pool, slowly, and as you get your head under and wave to the underwater people you know—your wife, her old friends and their kids you realize something's strange; you feel different."

"You fuck," she spat; and he nodded.

"Marko always enjoyed me talking about Kline and Pollock and all the Cedar Bar stories, and he listened close to my opinions and perceptions, he was always interested to hear what I was writing about (or trying to write), or what I was drawing, or not painting, in fact it was all we ever talked about, and I of course loved it."

"Because you could talk about yourself."

"Right; you were sitting beside him and he was asking me about my new book; I felt something was funny, and you were always talking about psychology, I remember how he listened to you, and you listened to him while I sat there and got drunk, occasionally chattering about something, or the kids would start to whoop away, or his wife would suddenly want to play a record. I liked his eyes, I liked his power of listening, I liked his objectivity and I really admired the slow expansion of his pupils, 'real analyst's eyes,' I thought. And he seemed to understand from his listening distance, but like any guy, he didn't as much as I thought. Marko was generous with his patience, it was his style. He was a soft spoken, very perceptive and sensitive man who cared a great deal about people. He was very very patient, and controlled.

"But—something needled me. What was it? I kept asking myself. Then, when I called them, and asked them to meet us in the park, something clicked.

"Sherry answered the phone and in a distance I could hear—

a silence before she spoke— I neard a wind, and I softly said, 'Sherry?' There was a soft mumble, or cough. I said her name, again, gently, and she responded in a strange mechanical echo —'Yes?'

"I said who I was, and why don't we get together; it's a lovely day.

"She said, that, stop whisper, sounded, stop whisper, good, I heard her trying to come forward from it; the word good was desperate. I asked her where Marko was.

" 'He's—here,' she whispered, and after 'here' was nothing, a void, where was 'here'? I was tense, looking at it.

"Then I saw him. He was sitting on the sofa, across the city from me, across the living room from Sherry as she talked to me on the phone. Her back was to him, and he was looking at her—no, watching her, and his pupils were expanded, giving him a hard, cold look—a terrible look, with his beard, a direct satanic look of fury and impatience.

" 'Wait a second," she said, in a strangled voice, and I saw her turn to him. She trembled under the power of his eyes, and he changed them.

" 'Who is it?' he asked.

"She told him, and about Central Park. I heard him be enthusiastic, and saw his face brighten.

"We arranged the place to meet.

"We met them at the zoo, we had a pleasant afternoon.

"We asked them to come down to our loft for supper, and they thought that was a fine idea, but their car was so full of furniture, for some reason, they couldn't give us a ride down, and just before they got in their car, and just before we turned to head for the subway, Marko looked at you. Do you remember how he looked at you?"

"Yes. I don't want to. Why are you doing this?"

"Please let me go on. You loved him then, and now, out of the past, he was unlocking the car door, Sherry at his side gazing up at him, but Marko's eyes were on you, hard, they drilled across space into yours, as I stood beside you watching him. He was trying to tell you—and in that still air of an October Sunday afternoon, Sherry, in a shattering whisper, pathetically asked, 'Why don't you ever look at me like that?'

"Marko didn't even turn to her. He answered—and could we have heard correctly, on that strange still afternoon air?

" '*Because she's prettier than you are.*'

"They got into their car swiftly. We took the train down, and met them at the door and came up here. I went to the delicatessen and we had Sunday afternoon beer and cold cuts, and it was very tense. I gave the kids paper and crayons and charcoal so they could draw, and then, just before they all left—it was—I couldn't stand knowing something I wasn't conscious of—I had had a quart too much of beer, and I amost took him by the lapels, and said anxiously, it was *very* I repeat *very* important that he come by where I work, and see me! Marko was a little astonished, and, as he was and is a deep man, I saw his eyes were telling me I was trying to tell him something.

" 'What is it? What is it?'

"It was clicking through my mind, dot dash dot dot dash I couldn't translate it, it didn't get through, they left, and a week later the phone call came which sent you weeping out of your head into my arms: Sherry had jumped to her death."

"I arrived at the funeral parlor before you did. Marko was in the inner lobby. I shook his hand solemnly, and expressed regrets. His eyes were in terrible emotion, and then you came in, like something off the *Saturday Evening Post* cover you went straight into his arms. He wholly embraced you, and wept in your presence.

"You and Marko talked a while, some of your old friends showed up out of childhood, and time dragged around. I got a drink of water and when most of the people had left in the inner parlour, I went in.

"I was confused, and of course felt alarm. I hate those places. But—and as I trembled I knew I would experience something which would reward me, and one more thing would fall into place—I went in on a string, I went down the aisle, I moved toward the casket with death all decked out around me, obliquely, across my life, and then I was there.

"I looked down at her waxen face. I was so right I felt faint, dizzy with it. Her eyebrows were raised sharply arched, and her eyes were so severely closed, and her lips so tight it was as if, an inside job, they had been sewn shut and it had a nasty twist, a shattering bitterness, a mock smile—she had made it, the one shot leap had worked; it had been her triumph.

"I set my teeth in rage and helplessness. The head on the silken pillow was a ravaged history, headlined:

REST
IN
PEACE

"I made a vow: in response to a question I didn't know, I vowed I would. *I will*, in revenge and heartbreak.

"Goodbye, sweetheart."

"About six months later we went to Marko's new apartment, and he was with his new woman. She was lovely. He was visibly happier, and he was now seeing patients. Remember when he showed us his office? But then we began to drink and things got bad. You hated me that night. I wanted to tell him I'd never forget Sherry, that he killed her and he *must* learn to live with it.

"How could that be true? But my emotions meant so much to me, and if he can't live with what he did, how can he understand that I do?"

It was bitter cold. The writer and his wife walked down the street holding hands. They had just come from a party.

He unlocked the door and let her in, he locked the door and they went up the stairs, and he opened the blue door into their loft, and the golden light from the far corner lamp shone outward as in Rembrandt, and the objects of their living had a sudden identity, he helped her with her coat and then she heated the coffee.

They drank coffee by the Christmas tree, eating the Christmas cookies her mother had made.

As they had arrived at the party—as they had just arrived Kingsley was leaving. They said hello. Kingsley was cool, and that was that, or that was that then, but when the writer and his wife had gotten in to the party, had taken their coats off, glad to be there and dance after a ruthless afternoon, the writer and his wife, really dancing, on a crowded floor to slam bang music, looked at each other and laughed, saying, together:

"Fate."

He walked across a rising field of ice.

He went up it. It was a mountain covered with ice, and he remembered Ronald Coleman at the end of the movie.

Was it the end of the movie?

It was bitter cold. But he felt an odd sentimentality sweep up and turn into sorrow, and then to grief, and he began to cry, weeping and struggling up the slippery ice field. He was weeping for himself, but he was going ahead! His heart beat faster, there was the ridge! He was actually going ahead! He was going toward—? What. The top? But there it was!

Down and down he fell, tumbled, rolling, all the way down the mountain in a swirl of snow and wind, he bumped against the base of a tree, and he lay confused in pine needles. A tall man in a uniform was standing there, and the tall man (it was the Christmas Officer), began to interrogate him.

The writer grinned.

"There I am working to get to Paradise only to wind up with you in the woods."

"Evidently you're not out yet," the man said.

"Why be so corny?"

"What's ice?"

"A field for dreams."

Great glacial barriers, frozen force of power larger than life. what was it? Ice was frozen water. They chased identities and associations without any luck.

"What about a force of resistance? As field equaling self, as I—experience, me going—crossing a way, a high way face, or a vertical ice wall —I have to break through."

"Break through the glacier?"

"To get to the mountain underneath . . ."

"Mountain? Underneath?"

"Or behind, an ice-wall in front of a mountain. I have to go over the mountain to get to—Rimbaud said you have to go through the mountain, not over it—well I was going over it to get to something."

The Christmas Officer smiled. "Paradise."

"—What—"

"Yet Rimbaud said you had to go through the mountain. Didn't you say ice covered mountain? No, mountain underneath, that was it."

"Yes, but to get to—"

"Who. What is the mountain underneath."

Power, power, a mountain of emotional power.

"The room is dark."

The universe was outside each ear—dot dot dash dot rigid in the chair. Time was incredible. The Christmas Officer had risen and the writer also, but woodenly.

Next session:

"Do you remember Grimm's fairytale about a ring? Yes, yes, sorry of course, etc., the king, I think the king is on an ice floe, it is dark and cold and the sea is stormy. He finds a ring in the ice. Something like that."

"The king?"

The writer blushed, and tears stung his eyes. He lowered his head. The Christmas Officer said,

"It's hard to accept, isn't it? You, king. King, also father, and it became difficult; well, we will get to it. But how can you be king when there is another? Who is that?"

"Father—my father was and always will be king. The most kingly kind of man."

"King*ly*. King*ly*. Why? Is it because you can't say you're king, in the face of your father, you are only—you feel your kingness in calling him kingly—even king—was and is and always will be, king, amen and yes. But actually you are king; the kingly kind, found even in your language. That is your truth, which is your fear."

The writer would not look at his interrogator, who said, "It hurts, so deeply."

The writer whispered, "Sure."

The Officer said, "It is almost impossible for you to confront your father and say, 'I am father' when you can't admit that now you are married you don't dare—be—"

"Me."

"Yes," the Officer said warmly. "Do you have any daydreams on this? There can be a lot there. Would you like to wait and think a bit, or continue."

The writer said he wanted to get to the ring. The Officer nodded, and the writer wiped his eyes.

"It's a wedding ring."

"How is your wife?"

"Ice and a ring." The writer added, bitterly, "Now how about that."

The Christmas Officer nodded.

The writer angrily said, "I was right. Experience as field of self. I can't believe it, don't want to." He covered his ears. The Officer frowned, what was.

The writer muttered, "Bells."

"Bells?"

"Bells! Conflict and anxiety!" the writer cried, "don't you see? I saw you nod! That means you saw! I've got the ring and I'm stuck on the fuckin' ice! ICE-cold—ICE!" He shouted, "Don't you GET IT?"

"Ah. Her."

"God-*damn* you and your classic understatements."

"What's Paradise."

The writer threw a look at the Christmas Officer snarling, "My wife and I together."

"She dropped her ring somewhere! Is *that* what you mean?"

The writer admitted: "Right in my path."

And put his head in his hands.

Going down the elevator it began to come to him. He was

(121)

snapping his fingers as he rapidly left the building. He ran to the subway.

She served the Chinese cooked beef over rice with brussel sprouts on the side. It was Sunday afternoon, outside quite cold in off and on sunshine. She said,
"I don't want to talk."
"I do," he said.
They looked at each other. He said, "When you withdraw from me now, I understand what I used to feel when I didn't understand. You see, I thought you were withdrawing to some-one else."
Her face was going through changes behind an artificial amusement. He said,
"Yet you insisted there was no one else, that my jealousy was crazy. There is no one, you said, and I believed you when you said you withdrew to be alone. You meant that then, but now we can realize, from your dream on Christmas Eve, that in fact you were, then and now, withdrawing from me to Marko."
She hesitated, then agreed. He said,
"Think of the seven years we've been together. Think of that. I haven't painted a picture in all that time. Well, the thing I experienced when you withdrew, even when I knew you were going into yourself, was, first, a deep and miserable chill —a shudder which turned into jealousy. Why? And how can cold create heat? Because you were cold, and I mean you were really cold to me. You were *ice* to me, and you made me jealous by turning, away from me to Marko."
"Yes, it's true," she whispered.
"You didn't know it, but when you told me you had a reward-ing talk with Kingsley (That! Of all the people! Of all the

names!), I experienced the old icy shudder which then became jealousy, but today—no, on Wednesday night it came clear, and I tell you my darling the dead are stirring in their graves. Yet none of it—not any of it—means anything to me if we can be really together. When you said there was no one, I wanted to believe you, yet you, as you stood before me, were more clear than your words, and it was a paradox, that you were there before me and you also were not, while your words were saying, 'alone, alone' but I knew there was another one."

She said, "I am cold to you when I do that, and you're right about Marko. I—I don't know what to do about it."

"I don't either!" His face was drained of blood as he whispered, "What made him do it, he must have *hated* her. Am I crazy?"

He gave her a long look. "Don't love Marko. Okay, you know him better than I do, but don't love him now, from then; I don't know why he and Sherry got married in the first place, but—they did. Did they ever go out? I mean to movies, or bars, or parties? I'll bet not. They had the baby of course, then, and Marko was working hard in school, and yes they were broke, all good excuses die in our own headlines. Can't be true, can it? No, can't be. But you love him from then, yes, which explains when I am the way I know you love me to be, you're guilty because you—you love me—but never completely, for out of the past comes Marko into your life, a figure of understanding and communication—as you flash your message of love across the floor to me, I see a shadow of guilt cross your wonderful self, I wondered why I hated you, and resented something. What was it? I kept asking myself, bitterly standing there at the bar, why should I go home? For what? To be with her? Why?" He looked at her sadly and angrily, or drunk, one eye was a little off. "Who can believe it? Who wants to?"

She was perfectly still.

"Well," he said, straightening his face, "we know, so you can approach your guilt directly, or more directly; because I love you."

Her head was lowered. "I'm going to cry."

"As I saw her being cold to me I saw her being warm with him, and knowing what Marko is to me, I felt double-crossed, and she suddenly became a rising figure of death in my mind, and I was frightened, faint and dizzy, in the whirlpool I told you about, but—"

"Wait. How about his wife, Sherry? What was she like?"

The writer clenched his fists—"I—I liked her, I felt a sympathy—afterwards—"

"After what."

"After I got to know her—or them, Marko and Sherry, she was impossible at first, almost hostile, blunt and caustic, friendly though, yet she was never—ever—close, and then, as we visited them more, I saw there was something, I didn't fully know, but she was, in a way, something terrific, to me; there was a hidden warmth and power of tension, nerves all going right and wrong at once that I almost envied, she seemed very alive, I liked her. Boy she was real! Did I think about sex? Maybe, but I always do, I felt—"

"Like a brother?"

"No. Like I could understand—that's it! I felt I understood her. We went out for beer once; Marko and my wife stayed in the apartment (check), well Sherry and I got the beer, and as we were going home—her hand was around my arm—I felt close to her. We stopped in a bar and had a couple of beers, but she didn't know—well, she didn't know what it was, I mean she didn't know where she was, or what was where she didn't know! It was a bar! A bar! She had never been in a bar! She sat beside me like something sad, cut from a party hat and turned into pulp, she sipped her beer, and she couldn't finish it; she couldn't talk. She stared ahead, she hadn't said a word. I finished my beer and hers and we left. On the way home she relaxed a little, not much, but a little, and I knew there was trouble. We went into the apartment, and there was Marko with my wife, just as we had left them, and it was something strange. Crazy-like a dream, it was always like a dream. I was there and I was not there, I was talking and drinking. What was happening? Anyway I began to like Sherry."

"You mean you fell in love?"

"Did I? Do you think so? No. But maybe."

"She would need you."

"Yes, but that's not what—"

"In a way you could care for her, she would need you."

"Yes, but—"

"Who—"

"Okay Goddammit, my wife, will you let me go on?"

"If your wife turns away she doesn't need you, and you can hardly care for her doing that, isn't that right?"

"Right, lots of fights over that."

"Okay, why don't you tell me about that—the fights, why deny your emotions? Nobody's saying need is love, but it's there," he paused. "Think a moment, how you are when you need your wife."

"Yes, that's good, and I see now—I do—but understand how I felt when I saw Marko's wife in the casket, her face—it was as if she was trying to tell me something, I can't say—exactly, as if she really didn't know either, but took it to the grave with her. I don't know! I CAN'T—somehow, *say* it! But I made a vow—and I didn't get it! I—I made a vow: *I will*."

(125)

The voice seemed to come out of Egypt:

"Do you know what it was?"

The writer, spellbound, shook his head. "No. I can't seem—to get—"

"*Remember me.*"

"*—God,*" the writer began to weep. "I will." Simply.

"Whether or not Marko killed Sherry—*that* is another story. The woman you thought would—could—need you, whom you cared for, is dead, surely the look on her face was one of revenge: she got Marko to pay attention to her at last, and tragically for him, too late. But as we haven't much—how long have you known your wife?"

"Seven years."

"Where did you meet her?"

"Provincetown."

"What were the circumstances?"

"Franz Kline asked me to help him fix up his summer house."

The Christmas Officer had a startled look. "I—when you were married, wasn't Kline the best man?"

"Yes."

"And didn't Kline die that same year?"

"Yes, that—the year we were married."

"Then how did you—"

The writer cried, "Don't even ask me! I know you by now! I was guilty!"

"When did you stop painting?"

"About—seven years ago—to find myself in language!"

The Officer leaned forward. "Since you met your wife! Now," and he said it intensely: "Tell me who it was who said *remember me.*"

The writer's hands began to shake. "What's painting got to do with it? I write now, I *must,* and I—I don't know, are you telling me I hate my wife? What is it? I love her—I do!" The Officer began to stand up. He had a harsh look on his face, and a hard perceptive demanding expression in his eyes, as the writer fumbled, "It seems, I think, or I feel a wild devotion, I say *I will*, with *all my heart*, my—"

"Darling." The face on the silken pillow.

"Oh God—*God*," the writer wept, openly, "it was my wife."

The Christmas Officer gravely nodded, and for a moment they were a tableau, and then the writer struggled to his feet, in tears, in the disciplined and poignant gaze of the doctor, who parted the curtains and opened the door, and as the writer left, rode the elevator down, walked through the lobby, and outside onto upper Park Avenue, he saw her rushing into Marko's arms. And the other lay in the casket.

THE SUN RISES INTO THE SKY

HIS WIFE got out of bed and dressed hurriedly. He rolled over still in the dream listening to his wife's exclamations about her being late for work. He sat up, and looked at her.

But captured by the dream, he slipped back down and under the covers, and fell asleep.

A monk sat on a high stool at a table by a window, in the corner of a cabin on the side of a mountain. The monk was writing in a black bound looseleaf notebook; it was a brilliant yet simple narrative. The monk felt heat of enthusiasm and chill of fear, and as he gazed at the few lines he had written he knew he was right, yet he also knew his narrative would cost him dearly, the evidence being on the page before him. Total knowing had never been so well written, it must be true. On that page. But knowing his fear, and failing courage, curiosity was real, and though it was forbidden, he turned the page *to see what would come next*.

The page, like a tombstone, was pushed over, and from out of bright whiteness, a virgin whiteness, a jagged black spider rose, and crouched, and held its stance, powerful and evil. It stirred, and made harsh scrapings gathering itself to move towards the hand on the table, and like a shadow it crept across the page, over the wood table top, and onto the monk's fingers, and as the monk's hand was up, and partly curved, the spider moved onto the monk's open palm, as the monk writhed, hand frozen, as if nailed down, he rocked back and forth and tossed his head, as the creature dug into the skin, and exuded in a terrible downward drive its darkness into the monk's hand and blood.

He woke in frenzy.

The second dream came around a week later, at about the same time. He woke as his wife was rushing to go to work, again almost late and complaining as he helped her find her keys, and gloves, and then after a hurried kiss she was gone.

The book in his hands was thicker. The writing was different than before—not so brilliantly clear, clear like something old made clear.

The cabin was clean; shelves were packed with books, the day was warm, or rather the dawn was warm, and he looked at his book.

The sentences ran across the pages and filled the book, they told a story, and he read his story and it was as though the pages were billowing curtains in front of large open doorways, and he felt a wind on his cheek as if tugging at a chill deep in his guts, like the residue at the bottom of a deep dark well, and he feared the words he had used, and he saw and felt a sense of stone; old stone, his Stonehenge: of emotion.

Madness, and a fearful joy filled the sentences. The man came out of the ground and filled the sentences as his son shuddered in written winds of violence and love of the dead, and the monk wrote *"it is colder,"* and pulled his threadbare robe around him and looked at the book, a small book getting larger, a gust of wind whipped up off the page—so cold he cried out.

Sunday they both had hangovers and it was a day then of a late breakfast, reading and napping and humor and loving; she

(129)

made a fantastic supper with chicken and onions and mush-rooms, noodles with a smoking butter/garlic sauce, and French stringbeans. It was so good they laughed as they ate. At mid-night she made cocoa. And they read late.

He was reading a novel by Nevil Shute, *An Old Captivity*, a really dreadful novel, which became worse and worse and he finally threw it across the loft, as his wife laughed; she had read it too. But the beginning of the book involved a dream by the pilot who had been hired to fly an archeologist to Greenland, and by air chart the whole area that the archeologist was dig-ging—something like that, and the way the author wrote about the plane, and the flying, was terrific. At first.

As the journey progressed, however, the pilot began to have strange dreams, and was unable to remember them the next day, it began to bother him more and more and when they got to Greenland and everything was set up the pilot couldn't sleep so had to take sleeping pills. One night he took three and the next day they couldn't wake him; one of the Eskimos said the pilot wasn't going to wake, ever, etc., and the pilot's feet began to get cold, very cold, and then his finger tips, etc., and then his heart slowed.

The Eskimos said they had better move him from this haunted campsite, etc., they did, and thirty six hours later the pilot woke up and the girl, the professor's daughter, took his hands, and he looked her square in the eyes and said he would ask Lief if they can stay, and the book slammed against the wall and fell to the floor.

"Yeah. I get it," he said, and began to work on one of his manuscripts, yet the written cold of Greenland prevailed, and so did the pilot figure who dreamed of his archaic past. He tossed and turned, and the lights went out. She fell asleep, and he stared at the ceiling. It was November, and the loft became chilly, and he tried to find a position to sleep in, and in his anxiety he began to perspire, and then literally water began to run down his face, and he began to be afraid he would catch cold, and slowly the loft got colder and colder.

"Lie still!"

He made a final attempt at comfort, pulled the covers close around him, and settled his body and began the effort of giving up consciousness; he wanted to sleep, and following the rules of that desire, in a passion to turn over a new leaf he began to sink, and having made contact with a good beginning in fiction, he began to relax in an outward spreading darkness, deeply, into the cabin with his book. The spider sprang up, alert, to be fed and to be charged in itself, and trembled on the snowy page, and the monk twisted in agony, and in terror, trying to move his paralyzed hand; a cold wind came in the window, it blew and chilled the monk—it came from a far place, and the barren cabin was cold, and yet within the fear and the chill, something was different. It lacked—

It lacked its former drama.

The spider leaped onto his wrist, NO the monk screamed, as the tiny needlepoint spider leg-tips claws dug in the skin above his pulse, and even as he groaned and rolled his eyes it was different, and gradually sensing a consciousness, he fought it, forcefully, and watched the evil black spider working down down to inject the darkness into him, it didn't work, it didn't and the spider paused and the monk stared in disbelief: the spider was impotent.

It was straining on the monk's wrist, it shuddered, and then, slowly, it began to shrink within itself, and become thin, and hardly able to move, staggered weakly to the edge of the monk's wrist, and tumbled off and fell into darkness.

His wrist was bare, the page was filled with sentences. The

monk rubbed his hands. The question of what would come next—was over.

A candle burned brightly on the desk. Books filled the shelves around him. A clock ticked to his right, and pens and paper, ink, and stacks of manuscripts lay in scattered sloping piles; the room was warm. The window was closed.

The air was still. The chill wind had gone.

The monk opened the window, and looked out. The wind receded across the valley, and across the mountains, and plains and hills far away, back; father was journeying back into the grave.

A hush fell over the mountain. The monk—the writer—I— read the sentences, and looked at the clock. It was my day off from work, in fact it was ten after four and my wife was due home: I had worked on my story all day—there were many stories to tell, and I would tell them and I would witness my past recede, and leave me alone to suffer my further emotions, greater surely, and therefore more terrible than any before, but as if in a dream—it came to me—incredibly, as the sun rises into the sky at the end of my dream distance was no longer an influence. Father. Even then, when he and it was, it and he was and were the past the size of the future, looming so huge, the massive mountain of *to be*—to be myself, be all of it my future, rising, into it all, willing, with him, we will move the tombstone into place, and name it the *Lapis*, and so realize the tone, like the sound of a call: of a new literature on our lips.

Bozo, old sweetheart,

Many developments have taken place since you went to go back to New York. The biggest, like I'm getting married. Yeah! To Leanne. For real, October 22 to be exact. Passing strange?

I've found a groove, the world has stopped its upside routine at least for a while.

Viz: I'm in love. I'm writing almost every night, and lush doesn't shove me around and snicker anymore. In short, I'm straight. Gigging on the wharf, longshoreing and over and above all, I'm off the phoney horseshit kick, that's been on my back for the last three or four years. I practice my trumpet again and it no longer sits in a forgotten corner sending out sorrowful vibrations on a deaf ear. And I dig it. All of it. Even the fact that I've admitted to myself that to do anything, I have to have a woman that really digs me, that in that sense, I'm hopelessly dependent on women to prove me a man to myself. That I am not the find em feel em fuck em hero that I tried to convince myself I saw every time I trimmed my beard. So for the first time in years I'm being honest to myself as well as forcing myself to be honest to people I meet and most of all (this the hardest part) the people I've already met.

Bozo, baby, I'm an excited cat! I control myself again, and O mother, it swings so much. I'm finding out now just how much I was actually hated by people in P-town this winter. When I reflect upon it I can't really blame them. I was pretty fucking hopeless; a real drag. All of a sudden I've got friends . . . . real friends. In the people I really wanted to be friends with, i.e. Tony Vievers, a lot of people that I think have something to offer. To produce. Like swingers. Something besides Zen Boom-di-di-boom-di-di-my life is a bowlofshit boomboometc. cocksuckers. Bozo I've learned the necessity of discrimination.

The summer was the epitome of shit. It drove me out of Old Colony life and into thought. And Leanne. We both had her pegged wrong, old dog. After she got away from that fucking Marylin idiot and got her own pad she became a different chick. Remember the basketball games that they used to broadcast in

New York, when some joker would score and the announcer would say, "There's a fast lay up, it circles the rim and it's . . . GOOD, like Nedicks." Well, that's the way it is with me, only it isn't a two point score. Put it this way. WOW, enough said.

Sue Chapp is getting married to an old friend of mine in D.C. All I'll say is that he is a groove, a damn fine writer. Porter Tuck got married too. This seems to be the fucking season for it.

So anyway, I saw Franz this morning and he said you and your old lady were swinging. Huzza says I. That's one scene that I really hope never quits, always wails . . . you darling wailing mother fucker.

Like be around the Cedars on the night of the 23 Oct. and we'll quaff awhile.

yeah, Pete

P.S. MAN, what a session I Blew with KONITZ while He was up here. Zoot Sims And I Didn't hit it off At All. Though I Tried. But KoniTz AND I Blew, BABY. Blew!

Printed November 1973 in Santa Barbara and Ann Arbor for the Black Sparrow Press by Noel Young and Edwards Bros. Inc. Design by Barbara Martin. This edition is limited to 1500 copies in paper wrappers; 200 hardcover copies numbered & signed by the author; & 26 lettered copies handbound in boards by Earle Gray, signed & with an original drawing by Fielding Dawson.

Photo: James O. Mitchell

Fielding Dawson began his career in 1949 at Black Mountain College where he was associated with such noted poets as Robert Creeley, Edward Dorn, Charles Olson and Robert Duncan. He is considered an important figure in the now famous Black Mountain poetry movement.

"What Dawson has is a spectacular sense of how people talk, & that gives him a sureness on the waves of communication — he can find in that ocean an utter fiction, make it be there for him & for us. I trust his ear more than that of any novel/ist now working."

ROBERT KELLY